# Red-Hot Hightops

# Red-Hot Hightops

## Matt Christopher

*Illustrated by* Paul D. Mock

Little, Brown and Company
Boston   New York   Toronto   London

First Paperback Edition

The characters and events in this book are fictitious. Any similarity
to real persons, living or dead, is coincidental and not intended by
the author.

Library of Congress Cataloging-in-Publication Data
Christopher, Matt.
    Red-hot hightops.
    Summary: Normally fearful to play basketball in front of a crowd,
Kelly becomes a confident and aggressive player when she dons a
mysterious pair of red sneakers that she finds.
ISBN 0-316-14056-2 (hc)
ISBN 0-316-14089-9 (pb)
    [1. Basketball—Fiction.  2. Sneakers—Fiction.
3. Mystery and detective stories]  I. Title.
PZ7.C458Rd  1987  [Fic]                        87-345

HC: 10 9 8 7 6 5
PB: 10 9 8 7 6 5
                       MV-NY

Published simultaneously in Canada
by Little, Brown & Company (Canada) Limited

Printed in the United States of America

to
*Dale,*
*Karen,*
*Kimberley,*
*and*
*Evan*

# Red-Hot Hightops

# One

"Shoot, Kelly! Shoot!"

The cry came from one of the Eagles' fans in the crowd that covered nearly every seat of the grandstand on the east side of the Eastburg Middle School gymnasium. A second later it was joined by another. "Don't just stand there, Kelly! Shoot!"

Kelly Roberts, her hands gripping the basketball in front of her, stared at the net that hung like a torn, limp rag some fifteen feet ahead. She was in the corner, with no Mockingbird player within yards of her.

But that weird feeling — that unexplainable fear that froze her every time she had an opportunity like this — gripped her again. Sweat drenched her face. Her heart beat a rapid tattoo. She just couldn't shoot.

Suddenly a girl in red swept in front of her, reached up, a̶̶tried to put her hand on the ball.

"Kelly! Here!" a familiar voice shouted.

The freeze that held Kelly thawed as she saw Ester Cabanis run up beside her. Kelly quickly bounced the ball to her. She caught it, rushed past the Mockingbird player, jumped, and shot.

The ball brushed the side of the glass board, struck the rim, wobbled around it a couple of times, then slithered through the net.

Applause exploded from the Eagles' fans. On the electric scoreboard, high up on the wall opposite the grandstand, the red lights of the score changed to read: Mockingbirds 43, Eagles 39. It was the last quarter.

"What's with ya, anyway?" Ester asked, as she and Kelly ran down the court together.

Kelly shook her head. The tight curls of her black hair swirled back and forth across her sweaty shoulders. "I don't know," she said. "It's the old problem — I keep freezing up. It's so embarrassing!"

"Well, look at it this way," Ester said, "you'd make a terrific model for some very patient artist."

"Fun*neee*," Kelly said.

"Cut the small talk!" Coach Tina Kosloski yelled over the hubbub of the fans' chatter. "Get into your positions!" The blonde Eagles coach was sitting on the bench with the team's subs, the gaze of her fiery blue eyes darting over the court, covering every move.

Carol Ames, the Mockingbirds' right guard, took out the ball, and in two quick passes Eadie Cornwall, their center, was dribbling it across the center line into their end of the court.

"Get up there, Kelly!" Janet Koles yelled. "Cover your guy!" Janet, the tallest girl on the team, was the Eagles' no-nonsense captain.

She had a white band wrapped around her forehead to keep her long hair from flying in her face.

Kelly, still sick from that freeze a minute ago, sprinted upcourt, searching for the tall blonde forward she was supposed to guard. In a minute, Kelly saw her . . . too late. Carol had whipped Casey Long a pass to the right of the keyhole. Taking just two steps toward the basket, Casey went up with it, shoved the ball against the boards, and sank it for another two points. Mockingbirds 45, Eagles 39.

An elbow jabbed Kelly lightly in the ribs. "Know what?" Fran Russo said. "If I didn't know any better, I'd say you had paid Coach to play. What are you *scared* of, girl?"

Kelly looked at the team's right forward, whose short, black hair made her look more like seventeen than thirteen. "I can't help it, Fran," Kelly admitted. "Don't you think I try? I *do*. Honest!"

"Boy! Did you see that redhead hanging onto my back?" a voice cut in behind them. "She practically tore my shirt off!"

6

Kelly and Fran looked over their shoulders at Marge Jackson, the Eagles' long-legged, spry left forward.

"And the ref never saw her?" said Fran.

"You didn't hear him call it, did you?" Marge snapped back.

Kelly laughed. Marge seemed to have more trouble on the team than anybody else. Sometimes more fouls, too.

This time Ester took the ball from out of bounds and tossed a looping pass to Janet, who had to jump to catch it. She dribbled upcourt, two Mockingbird players running along on each side of her. She crossed the center line, stopped abruptly as the two players swooped in front of her, and took a shot. The ball arced gracefully into the air toward the basket and sank through the net without touching the rim. Mockingbirds 45, Eagles 41.

*Why don't I have the nerve to do that?* a voice screamed inside of Kelly.

"Down, Kelly! Down!" Janet yelled, as June McKay took out the ball for the Mockingbirds.

Kelly rushed downcourt, realizing that Casey

was already sprinting toward the basket. A long, on-the-target pass to her could mean another basket unless Kelly could quickly close the gap. Carol caught June's throw-in pass, dribbled once, then heaved the ball down-court.

It was short. Kelly saw it come directly at her. All she had to do was jump a foot or so and catch it. . . .

"Nice going, Kelly!" Ester shouted. "Here!"

Casey stopped in her tracks. She was now rushing Kelly, her long legs and arms churning. Kelly saw her. Suddenly that terrible freeze feeling swept over her again.

"Get rid of it, Kelly!" Ester yelled.

Casey was almost on her now, reaching for the ball. Desperate, knowing she *had* to throw it now or lose it to Casey, Kelly heaved the ball past Casey's shoulder to Ester. It was a good pass. Ester caught it, dribbled it up-court, shot it to Janet, and bolted toward the basket at the same time. Janet took one dribble toward the basket, feinted a shot, then passed it back to Ester. Ester caught it with one hand

and went up with it for a two-pointer. The horn buzzed, ending the game. Mockingbirds 45, Eagles 43. "Well, at least we didn't get swamped," Fran said, as she headed off the court with Kelly and the rest of the team.

"Yeah. Right," Kelly said absentmindedly. She wondered if Anthony had been watching her. She hated to imagine what he must have thought of her playing. How could she ever get to talk to him? *Really* talk to him. They were lab partners in science, but they hadn't said more than two words to each other outside of class. She wanted to let him know that she liked him. And that maybe they could go to a school dance together sometime, or a movie. But no guy would want to go anywhere with a girl who froze up like a Popsicle on the court every time she got the ball.

The locker room seemed like a beehive as the girls swarmed into it. Kelly stopped in front of her locker, opened it, and started to reach for her towel when something caught her eye. A package. A red, oblong, gift-wrapped package tied with a red ribbon.

"What in — ?" she started to say. She took it out. On top of the package were a red bow and a typewritten note: *To Kelly. Good luck!*

Kelly's brown eyes widened. Her tar-black hair swirled about her shoulders as she looked around. Who was the wise guy who had put the package into her locker? And why? Her birthday was months away.

None of the girls was paying any attention to her. Not even her closest friend, Ester Cabanis. Ester was standing near the bench not far from Kelly, apparently too busy slipping out of her sweat-drenched uniform to be interested in what was going on around her.

Kelly turned back to the package and looked for a clue as to whom it might be from. There wasn't any.

She removed the wrapper to discover a white shoe box. She lifted the lid. Inside was a pair of brand-new, red hightop sneakers.

# **Two**

"Hightops?" Kelly murmured. "*Red* hightops, yet! Who *did* this?"

She looked again at the girls. Some of them were staring at her now — and at the red sneakers — with a dumb, innocent expression on their faces. Even Ester, a towel draped over her, noticed them by now.

"What have you got there?" she asked, popping her bubble gum.

"Look for yourself," Kelly replied. "Who put them in my locker? That's what I'd like to know."

"Not me," Ester said, her hazel eyes wide

11

as saucers as she stared at the sneakers. "Anyway, don't you lock your locker door?"

"Sometimes I do, sometimes I don't," Kelly said. "Who'd want to steal my clothes?"

She plunked down on the bench, blew out a gust of air, and glanced around at the team members. "Did one of you put these sneakers in my locker?" she asked quietly.

Everyone shook her head no.

"I can't believe it," Kelly said. "One of you *must* have."

"Why one of us?" Fran snapped. "We were all here together before the game started, and we all went out on the court together when it began. Somebody must have put them in there during the game."

"Guess you'll have to hire a private detective, Kelly," Ester said, blowing a bubble the size of a baseball before it snapped. "Anyway, now that you've got them, try them on. If they fit, great. If not, give them to somebody who can wear them."

Ester picked up one of the sneakers, peeked inside, and shook her head. "Not my size. Definitely. Too small."

12

Kelly removed her left sneaker and tried on the red one. It fit her!

"I don't believe it," she said. "They're perfect."

"Believe it," Ester said. "You've got a brand-new pair of hightops, kid. Thanks to a secret friend."

Kelly shook her head, then stuck the sneakers back into their box, undressed, and took a shower. When she was ready to go, she rewrapped the box with the red paper and carried it, along with the duffel bag holding her sweaty uniform, out to the parking lot. What else *should* I do with the sneakers? she thought.

Her mother and father were already waiting for her. They were sitting in the car with her fifteen-year-old brother, Derek, and her eight-year-old sister, Valerie.

"What've you got there?" Mrs. Roberts asked, staring at the package Kelly was holding under her arm.

"You've got to see it to believe it," Kelly said, as she sat down on the back seat. She unwrapped the shoe box again, took out the

13

sneakers, and held them up for the whole family to see.

"Hey! They're neat!" Valerie cried. "Who gave them to you?"

"That's what's so funny," Kelly said. "I don't know."

"You don't know?" her father echoed.

Kelly looked at him in the rear-view mirror. He was sitting behind the wheel, but even in the shadows his black hair and brown eyes were clearly visible. "No, I don't," she said. "Someone left them in my locker with just a note saying *To Kelly. Good luck*."

"Did you ask Tony?" Derek asked quietly.

"Anthony? No. Why should I?" Kelly paused. "He wouldn't do a thing like that, anyway."

"You sure?"

"I'm sure. He . . . he has no reason to."

Valerie cleared her throat and giggled.

My big mouth, Kelly thought. I just mention him around the house a little, and those two talk as if we're going steady.

About an hour before lunch the next day, Ester came over. She lived at 131 Hawthorn,

14

in the college section. Her father was a professor. The two girls played one-on-one basketball with Derek's ball and the basket Mr. Roberts had put up on the front of his garage.

"You know what gets me?" Ester said, as Kelly reached out and stole the ball from her. "When we play here together — you and me — you play like a whiz kid. But on the court, you freeze like an icicle. What's the scoop?"

Kelly dribbled twice toward the basket, leaped, and sank a lay-up.

She looked at Ester and shrugged. "Don't ask me. I've been trying to figure that out myself."

As long as she could remember she had been shy. Not only on the basketball court, but off of it, too. What made her like that? Wish I knew, she thought.

"Did you find out anything more about the red hightops?" Ester asked.

"Nothing. Somehow, I don't expect to, either."

"No, I suppose not," Ester agreed. "Whoever gave them to you would have spoken up by

15

now, right? You going to wear them at the next game?"

Kelly shrugged. "I don't see how I could. You know we're supposed to wear white ones."

"Aw, Kosloski will let you. And who knows, maybe a change of sneakers will make a change in you."

Kelly laughed. "That would be something, wouldn't it?" she said.

She got the ball, tossed it to Ester, then rushed between Ester and the basket, jumping to keep her friend from making a shot. Suddenly Ester pivoted, swung around Kelly, and headed for the basket. Quickly Kelly reached out, grabbed the ball before Ester could dribble again, and took a set-shot. In!

Ester stared at her, and shook her head. "I'm telling you," she said, "you're really an animal. But here only. On the court you're a frozen banana."

"You have to rub it in?" Kelly said. "I *know* what I do." She got the ball, rolled it onto the grass next to the driveway, then fell onto the cool grass herself. "I've got a notion to quit

16

the team," she said, looking up at the blue, cloud-speckled sky. "Maybe I should. I'm dead weight. I'm holding you guys down."

"Don't be stupid," Ester said, dropping to her knees beside her. "You'll get over it."

"Sure. When I'm ninety."

"What're you going to do if you quit?" Ester asked. She took a stick of bubble gum out of her pocket, unwrapped it, and popped it into her mouth. "Want one?"

Kelly shook her head no. "Learn to spell so I can play Scrabble and beat the pants off Val," she said. "I haven't beat her since Mom bought us the game."

Ester laughed. "That's *it?* Just to learn to spell so you can beat your sister?" She started to chew her gum so loud Kelly could hear her.

"I'm a slow learner," Kelly said. "It'll probably take me all summer to learn some good, real long words."

Ester popped her gum. "Know your trouble?" she said. "You haven't got any guts."

Kelly stared at her. "Ester, that's a rotten thing to say."

"I know. But it's true." Ester rolled over onto her back and looked at the sky. "Know what else? Maybe you ought to wear those red hightops in the next game," Ester said. "Maybe they really will help you play better."

"Don't be funny."

"Try it," Ester said. "Since they fit, you haven't got a thing to lose, have you?"

"And nothing to gain," replied Kelly. She closed her eyes and yawned. "I'm a case," she said. "It would take a lot more than a dumb pair of sneakers to turn me into a better basketball player."

"Wish somebody would put a pair of new sneakers into my locker," Ester said. "You can bet your pj's *I'd* wear them."

# Three

On Thursday evening the Eagles played the Roadrunners, who looked sharp in their green, white-trimmed uniforms. It was the Eagles' fourth game of the season, their record standing at no wins, three losses. Kelly wished she could find out just once, at least, how it felt to be a winner.

Would wearing the red sneakers make a difference? she wondered briefly. What a joke. She only wore them to prove to Ester that Ester was bananas herself.

Both teams tossed practice shots at their baskets before the game got under way. Now

19

and then Kelly glanced at the stands to see where her family was sitting. She finally saw them — her parents and Derek and Valerie — sitting halfway up and near the center.

Was Anthony somewhere there, too? The fourth time she looked she finally spotted him, secretly admitting to herself that she had looked for him first, her family second. Most of the kids called him Tony, but she liked the sound of Anthony better. It was more, well — sophisticated.

After the warm-up, Coach Tina Kosloski gave the girls her usual briefing that was supposed to charge them up with lots of pep and vinegar. For some reason, though, it didn't seem to do any good. It hadn't helped in the first three games, and probably wouldn't in this game, either. But, you never know, Kelly thought.

The coach was tall and slender, with a short haircut and eyes that could scare you even if she had no intention to. "Don't let those girls with that three-one record intimidate you," she said. "Just tell yourself you're better than they are, and you'll find out that you are." *We've heard that before*, Kelly mused. "Okay. Get out there and show 'em. You hear?"

"We hear!" the girls answered almost in one voice, and the starting five ran out onto the court amid loud cheering and clapping from the Eagles' fans.

Janet lost the tip to Sue Courtney, the Roadrunners' five-foot-ten center, who quickly passed it to her left forward. In three passes the ball was close to the Roadrunners' basket. After a half-dozen tries, Sue finally laid it in. Roadrunners 2, Eagles 0.

Wonder how long I'll sit here before she puts me in, Kelly thought. It was the same thought she always had while sitting on the bench. Sometimes it was for two minutes. Sometimes longer. You never knew about Coach Kosloski.

Kelly glanced down at the shiny red high-tops. As Ester had predicted, the coach had said she could wear them, since they matched the Eagles' red uniforms. Thinking about them now made her skin prickle. Who *was* the person who had put them in her locker, anyway? And why the secret about them?

"Okay, Kelly. Take Ethlyn's place," the coach's voice interrupted her thoughts.

Kelly straightened up, nervous but excited. Maybe she'd never be a great basketball player, but that wouldn't keep her from loving the game.

She was in about twenty seconds when she saw Bea Talman dribbling in for a lay-up, and raced in toward the red-haired left forward. Just as Bea was going up for the shot, Kelly reached her and went up, too, raising her hand to deflect the shot from going into the basket. Instead, she struck Bea's elbow, causing the ball to deflect against the backboard.

The referee's whistle shrilled, resounding throughout the gym, and Kelly turned to see the bald man in the zebra-striped uniform pointing at her with his right hand and lifting two fingers of his left.

"Watch it, Kelly!" Janet cried.

Kelly stared at her, then at the ref as he got the ball and stepped toward the foul line.

"Two shots," he said.

Bea missed the first shot, but dropped the second one through the net without the ball's touching the rim.

"Take it out, Kelly," Janet ordered.

The ref tossed Kelly the ball, and she stepped behind the sideline. It took only two seconds for her to see Janet out there near center court, leaping and reaching skyward with those long arms of hers. Kelly, holding the ball above her head with both hands, leaped and whipped it over the heads of the Roadrunners' guards, directly into Janet's waiting hands.

Janet passed it upcourt to Marge, who dribbled it toward the corner and stopped to make a set shot. A Roadrunner swooped in front of her and blocked the shot, but Kelly intercepted it. Two Roadrunners popped in front of her almost at the same time, both getting their hands on the ball, trying to steal it from her.

Frantic, she yanked the ball away from them, dribbled toward the sideline, then paused, holding the ball in front of her.

"Way to go, Kelly!" a fan shouted.

24

She could feel everyone's eyes on her, waiting for her next move. The basket was some twenty feet away, a long distance. Too long for her to try a shot, she thought.

She saw Fran Russo cut in front of a Roadrunner guard and quickly bounced the ball to her. Fran grabbed it, dribbled toward the basket and went up with it in a high, graceful leap. The ball left her hand in a smooth glide, brushed against the glass backboard, and dropped through the net.

"Nice shot, Fran!" Kelly yelled, as the crowd exploded with an enthusiastic cheer.

"Thanks to you," Fran said, smiling as she ran up alongside of Kelly.

"Suppose it's those red sneakers?" Marge cut in, coming up on the other side of Kelly.

Kelly puffed at a strand of hair that had fallen across her face and smiled. "Yeah, sure."

How ridiculous! That Marge! Being a science fiction fan sure made her think up the wildest ideas. I'm basically a shy person, Kelly thought. I'm just determined to get over it, that's all.

Roadrunners' ball out. Bea Talman got it

and dribbled it across the center line upcourt. She was on the opposite side of the court from Kelly, and no one was in front of her.

Kelly buzzed across the court, running diagonally so that she'd be in a position to intercept the redhead near the Roadrunners' basket. Keeping her eyes steadily on Bea, she never saw the other player in green and white get in her path. Kelly rammed right into her. For a moment, stars danced in front of her eyes.

She waited till her head cleared, started to get up, then paused to stare at the girl she had run into.

It was Kate Ballenger, the Roadrunners' right forward. She lay sprawled on her side, her right leg lying straight out, her left knee bent, her eyes closed. Pain was etched on her face.

"Kate!" Kelly cried, kneeling beside her. "I'm sorry! Are you all right?"

Kate's eyes opened. She looked up at Kelly, then glanced away.

# Four

Ethlyn, a tall, green-eyed girl with a thatch of red hair, took Kelly's place at right guard.

"Hey, what am I seeing out there? A new girl?" Coach Kosloski asked, as Kelly came running in to the bench. A broad grin was on the coach's oval face.

"I didn't mean to run into her," Kelly said, apologetically. "I never saw her."

"I know you didn't. I'm talking about something else."

Kelly frowned. "About what?"

Coach Kosloski grinned. "Never mind. Just

27

keep playing the way you've been playing. That's all."

"Oh — that?" Kelly laughed.

She picked up one of the towels strewn on the bench, wiped the sweat off her face, and sat down. She thought of her parents and of Anthony, wondering if they had noticed her change of pace, too. Was it really as noticeable as the coach and some of the girls were trying to make her believe?

Ethlyn threw a long pass across the court that was intercepted by a Roadrunner who, seconds later, dropped it into the basket. Roadrunners 18, Eagles 15. When the clock read 2:28, Coach Kosloski ordered Kelly back onto the court and Ethlyn off.

Fran, her short, black hair shining, took out the ball from below the Roadrunners' basket and tossed it to Janet. Janet dribbled upcourt. As she crossed the center line she shot a pass to Marge, who took a few steps with the ball toward thc basket, then started to dribble it.

*Shreeek!* sounded the referee's whistle. <u>Kelly</u> saw the ref whirling his hands: the walking violation.

Kate took the ball out for the Roadrunners — Kelly was glad to see that the fall had not hurt her — and passed it to Sue. Sue quickly passed it upcourt to a teammate racing toward the Roadrunners' basket. But Kelly, seeing the play forming, was already sprinting upcourt, too. She got to the ball a fraction of a second before it reached Bea, snatched it out of the air, and dribbled it back toward her own basket.

"Kelly! Here!" came a cry from near the basket.

Kelly saw Ester running toward it from the opposite side of the court. But a Roadrunner was close behind her, and another was between her and Kelly. Kelly knew that only a perfect throw would make her sure of Ester's catching the ball.

She picked out a spot ahead of the tall left guard and heaved the ball. It shot across the court exactly where she wanted it to go. Ester reached for it, got her hands on it — then *dropped* it.

"Ohhh!" the Eagles' fans groaned.

The Roadrunner closest to Ester snatched the ball, pivoted, and passed it over her head to a teammate. Two seconds later the scoreboard lit up with another two points for the Roadrunners, putting them in the lead, 20–15.

Ester shook her head as she ran alongside of Kelly up the court. "Good pass," she said. "Sorry I missed it."

Kelly shrugged. "I threw it too hard. Forget it."

The Roadrunners continued their hot streak, making the most of the final minute and a quarter. They scored two baskets and a foul shot — the foul by Fran when she charged into a Roadrunner about to catch a pass — and the score went up, 25–15.

I don't believe this, Kelly thought. They can't be *that* good. But the scoreboard was proof.

Fran took out the ball, leaped, and passed

it over the head of the Roadrunner guarding her. Kelly didn't look to see who the intended receiver was. She didn't have time. But she could see that the coast would be clear ahead of her if she got the ball.

She sprinted forward, grabbed the pass practically out of the hands of the intended receiver, and dribbled it upcourt toward the basket. About ten feet from the basket a Roadrunner bolted in her path, stopping her dead in her tracks.

"Here!" Marge yelled.

Kelly, pivoting on her left foot, saw Marge heading for the basket and bounce-passed the ball to her. Like a flash, Kelly's guard stuck out her foot, deflecting the ball out-of-bounds.

It was then when Kelly turned and saw the distraught look in Ester's eyes and realized that it was *she* to whom Fran had intended to pass.

"Sorry about that, Ester," Kelly said.

Ester shrugged, said nothing. She's peeved, Kelly thought. She thinks she would have scored a basket if she'd gotten the ball. Well, maybe she would have and maybe she wouldn't. I'm not going to worry about it.

The horn blasted, ending the first half. Kelly joined the rest of the team as they trotted off the court, heading for the locker room.

She looked up into the stands — at Anthony. Their eyes met, held for just a few seconds. Blushing, Kelly looked away. If he would at least wave! she thought.

"Kelly! Wait!" he suddenly called to her as she continued on her way.

She stopped abruptly, turned, and saw him bouncing down the seats of the gym in her direction.

"Hi!" she said as he jumped off the bottom seat, landing close to her. Her heart drummed.

"Hi," he said. His smile deepened a small scar in his left cheek. "You're playing like a real pro out there. I mean . . . you're not acting like the scared kid you usually seem to be." He pointed at her sneakers. "Those snazzy red hightops wouldn't have anything to do with it, would they?" he added, chuckling.

She laughed. "That's what everyone keeps asking."

"They're new, aren't they?"

"Yes, I just got them. Actually, someone gave them to me," she said.

"Really? Who?" he asked offhandedly.

"I don't know. . . ." Kelly answered, eyeing him carefully. But he didn't look guilty, and she didn't have time to explain. "I've got to go, or Coach Kosloski will be wondering what happened to me. See ya."

She turned and started to head out of the gym — thinking, that was the first time we talked about something besides homework — when suddenly a girl she'd never seen before looked up at her from the drinking fountain.

"Hi, Kelly," the girl said, straightening up and wiping her mouth. "You're really playing a great game out there."

"Thank you," Kelly said.

Kelly observed the girl to be about her own height and build. Blue, tear-drop earrings hung down on either side of her pretty, heart-shaped face.

"I'm Sandi Hendrix, Phyllis's cousin," she explained.

"Phyllis Michaels?" Phyllis, tall, black-haired, and quite pretty herself, usually substituted for Janet. Ever since her parents had died in a car wreck a few years ago she'd been living with her aunt and uncle.

"Uh-huh," Sandi Hendrix muttered. "For a kid *our* size you're really doing great. I guess size doesn't really mean much if you've got what it takes, right?"

"I guess," Kelly said, not sure what to make of this girl.

Sandi cracked a smile, revealing perfectly white teeth. "Well, see you. And keep playing great basketball, okay?"

"I'll try," Kelly said, and watched the girl turn and head up into the stands. At least *she* didn't say a word about my red sneakers, Kelly thought as she headed out of the gym. Then again, Sandi what's-her-name could've thought I've *always* worn them, Kelly concluded.

Shrugging off any more thoughts about the girl, Kelly raced down the concrete stairs and into the locker room where all eyes were upon her the minute she entered.

"Well, Miss Roberts," Coach Kosloski greeted her from the other side of the room, "it's about time you showed."

Kelly blushed. "I'm sorry. I met someone. I didn't think we talked very long."

"*Whom* did you meet?" Janet asked, grinning like the Cheshire cat. "Your tall, dark, and handsome?"

Kelly met her eyes. Her mouth tightened.

"Okay. Enough," Coach Kosloski cut in. "I've got a few words to say before we go back on the court for the second half, so listen, and listen good."

Kelly turned to the coach, then sat down and unlaced her sneakers. Her feet felt hot and tired. She wished she could stick them into a pail of cold water.

# Five

The second half started differently than the first half. It was Marge who took the initiative. She grabbed a rebounder from a Roadrunner, dribbled the ball all the way up the court to the opponent's basket, then tossed a pass to Kelly, who was running up beside her. Kelly leaped and sank a lay-up without the ball's touching the rim.

Roadrunners 26, Eagles 17.

"Good going, Kelly!" shouted a fan.

"Nice play, guys!" Janet Koles said.

Marge smiled at Kelly. "Those red sneakers must be magic," she quipped.

Kelly laughed. "Yeah!"

36

Magic? Hah!

But she *was* playing better with them on, she thought. Wasn't she?

Thirty seconds later she was racing alongside of Kate Ballenger, who was dribbling the ball downcourt, and realized that Kate was surely going to get a good shot at her basket if she wasn't stopped.

Should I stop her? Kelly thought. She had to decide — now.

Before another second passed, Kelly rushed forward and gently pushed her.

Shreeek! shrilled the referee's whistle. "Pushing!" yelled the ref. "One shot!"

Kate made the point.

Roadrunners 26, Eagles 17.

"That's okay, Kelly! You're doing fine!" a male voice said from one of the lower seats beside her as she stood close to the sideline, waiting for the throw-in from Marge.

She glanced over her shoulder and recognized a familiar, smiling face. Oh, no, she thought. *He* couldn't have said that. Not Brett Williams. He doesn't even *know* me.

But the broad-shouldered, handsome blond

37

who played fullback for the football team and had scored more touchdowns last fall than anybody else *was* the guy who was looking and smiling at her.

She looked away from him, suddenly overwhelmed by the sound of his voice calling her name. *I don't believe it!* she thought. *He actually spoke to me! Brett Williams!*

"Kelly!" a voice shouted.

From the corner of her eye she saw the ball coming at her. Quickly she raised her hands to catch it. It came at her fast — so fast that it struck the side of her face and glanced toward the sideline, where one of the fans intercepted it.

The whistle shrilled.

"Green's ball!" the ref shouted.

Kelly stood crouched, her hand pressed against the side of her face. It felt like a hot iron and stars still popped in front of her closed eyes.

Someone put an arm around her. "Kelly! Are you hurt?"

She recognized Coach Kosloski's husky but tender voice.

38

"I'm okay," she murmured.

The stars faded. She opened her eyes. The pain was still there, but not as severe.

"Come on. Sit it out for a while," the coach advised, and led her off the court.

A smattering of cheers rose from the crowd. Kelly saw someone's long legs step aside from in front of her, and she looked up into Ester's worried eyes. But Ester said nothing and turned and ran down the court.

During the next few minutes Janet scored four points, and Marge three when she was fouled while trying a lay-up shot. The Road-runners picked up two. Roadrunners 28, Eagles 24. The Eagles' fans were shouting like mad. One of them — Kelly knew it was that crazy McFall kid — had a horn and blatted it every time an Eagle sank one in.

The score went up to 38–37 in the Road-runners' favor, when a Roadrunner accidentally kicked the ball out-of-bounds and Coach Kosloski said, "Okay, Kelly. Take Tootie's place. Report first!"

Tootie Davis was a substitute who seldom shot and seldom scored, but played well on

39

defense despite her size. She was twenty pounds overweight, but Kelly admired her ambition and had often wished *she* were like Tootie in that respect.

It's strange, Kelly thought. But, in this game, it seems that I really am. I can *feel* it.

"Sorry, Tootie," Kelly said as she went in.

"That's okay," Tootie said, sweat rolling down her face. "I'm pooped, anyway."

Fran took out the ball and passed it to Janet. Janet relayed it to Kelly. Kelly glanced around, saw no one between her and the basket, and went for it. She had hardly taken four steps when Sue Courtney, the Roadrunner's tall, quick center, got in front of her. Sue put both of her hands on the ball and tried to yank it loose from Kelly's strong grip.

Kelly yanked the ball hard, pulling Sue forward to the floor.

The whistle shrilled. "Jump ball!" barked the ref.

Sue rubbed her knees as she got slowly to her feet, her eyes burning into Kelly's.

"Sorry about that," said Kelly.

"I bet you are," Sue murmured.

"I really am," Kelly insisted. "I didn't mean . . ."

The ball went up. The girls jumped. Sue got the tap off to Bea Talman. But, in a move that seemed to surprise Bea and everybody else, Kelly got the ball, dribbled it out of the traffic, then shot a long pass upcourt to Ester who was waiting under the Eagles' basket. Ester caught it and sank it easily.

The horn blew seconds later, ending the third quarter. Roadrunners 38, Eagles 39.

"Come on! Come on!" Coach Kosloski urged her players, as she crouched down in front of the Eagles' bench.

Quickly the girls surrounded her. "We're only one point ahead," the coach reminded them, looking from one sweat-shiny face to the next. "We've got to keep that lead. You're proving that they are *not* number one. You are better than they are already."

Maybe this time her words were working, Kelly thought.

The fourth and last quarter started moments

later, with the Roadrunners scoring the first basket, a twenty-footer by Sue Courtney. Kelly took the ball out for the Eagles and less than three seconds later caught a short pass from Fran and dribbled it upcourt, stopping just past the center line where two Roadrunners blocked her. She pivoted back and forth on her left foot, faking a throw, feinting a shot to the basket, each time causing the girls to jump wildly, their legs spread-eagled, their arms shooting skyward.

Finally, out of the corner of her eye, she saw Ester glide past her guard toward the basket. Kelly shot the ball to her, bouncing it *through* the legs of one of the girls. Ester caught the pass, dribbled toward the basket, then went up with it. In!

"Nice play, Kelly!" a voice yelled above the din. It was Brett's. Kelly knew she would never forget the sound of it.

The Eagles sank in more baskets, three to every two of the Roadrunners'. Then, with a minute and a half to go, Kelly rushed an opponent who was heading for a lay-up shot. She went up with her, missed hitting the ball, but struck the girl's arm instead. The shot missed, too.

The whistle shrilled. "Pushing!" yelled the ref.

The girl made the foul shot. But one point was better than two, Kelly thought.

For the Roadrunners it was far from being enough. The Eagles walked off the court with their first victory, 51–45.

As Kelly left the court amid the proud and shouting Eagles fans, she heard a now-familiar voice say to her, "Nice game, Kelly."

It was Brett again. She smiled. "Thanks," she said.

He stepped in front of her, his cheerful green eyes peering at her. "How about a Coke one of these days? Or an ice cream?"

"Sure," she said, feeling slightly dazed.

She slipped past him. As she neared the locker room door she glanced back. He was still there, looking at her. But someone beyond Brett was looking at her, too. Anthony Fantella.

Her smile faded. She glanced from Anthony to Brett, then made a hasty dash into the locker room.

She sat down on the bench in front of her locker and wiped her sweaty face with a towel. No doubt about it, Anthony had seen her talking with Brett. Does he like me at all? she wondered. Maybe he's just as shy as I am about saying it.

She heaved a sigh, took off the red hightops, and started to place them in her duffel bag when a small, folded sheet of paper inside the bag caught her eye. Surprised, she picked it up, unfolded it, and read the typed note: "Please leave the sneakers."

What was going on? Were these her sneakers or not?

Just then a voice broke in. "Hi, Kelly. Hey! For a shy little runt you did all right!"

Kelly's eyes popped open wide. Sandi Hendrix was standing there looking at her straight in the eyes, smiling.

# Six

Sandi moved on, caught in the stream of girls entering the locker room. Kelly watched her retreating back, her own face red with anger. Her thoughts suddenly scrambled as she watched the girl stop, pause for a moment, then head toward her cousin, Phyllis Michaels.

Shy little runt, indeed! The nerve! How *dare* Sandi say that to me?

Kelly was even more taken aback the next day when Sandi came to the house alone. Kelly couldn't believe it. What was she going to do?

Apologize for calling me a shy little runt? she thought. Kelly was prepared to forgive her, when Sandi explained: "Phyllis had things to do and had to do them by herself. I didn't ask her what those things were, didn't think it was any of my business. Anyway, *I* didn't have anything to do, so I thought I'd pay you a visit," she added, her black eyes sparkling.

Kelly looked at her, dumbfounded. Obviously this creature, though she's no bigger than I am, doesn't even realize how she hurt me by calling me a shy little runt! Kelly thought. I ought to slam the door in her face!

"Sandi! Come in!" a voice cried out from behind Kelly. Valerie shoved Kelly aside and stepped across the threshold. She grabbed Sandi's hand and pulled her into the house.

"Wow! At least *someone* appreciates my unannounced visit!" Sandi said, laughing.

Kelly was too stunned by her younger sister's enthusiastic welcome to say anything for a moment. When had those two gotten acquainted, anyway? She forced a smile as she closed the door. "Sorry. I didn't mean to be

rude. Val just surprised me by her bubbling welcome, that's all. As if you were a long lost friend she'd just found again."

"We met at the game yesterday," Val explained, her large brown eyes framed by the loose strands of her long, black hair. "She sat with us."

Kelly arched her eyebrows. "Oh?"

Sitting with Val and her parents? And Derek?

She heard familiar footsteps approaching and saw Sandi's eyes light up brightly.

"Hi!" Sandi greeted Derek.

"Hi," he replied. "Nice to see you again!"

Kelly stared at her red-haired, older brother. Derek was tall and muscular. She could see why he attracted girls, but he and Sandi had met only the night before, and now Sandi was coming here, apparently without invitation. . . . Well!

Seconds later, Mrs. Roberts — her red hair done up as if she were ready to go out — came into the living room, wiping her hands on a dishcloth.

"Sandi! What a pleasant surprise!" she exclaimed, greeting the visitor with almost the same enthusiasm that Valerie had. "Have a seat. Would you like something to drink? A glass of orange juice, maybe?"

"No, thanks," said Sandi. "I haven't been up long, and I had a big breakfast."

Kelly looked at Sandi's lean figure — noting the ever-present tear-drop earrings hanging from her earlobes — and thought: How big? Four spoonfuls of cornflakes and a glass of milk?

It took Kelly less than thirty seconds to realize that Sandi hadn't come here to spend time with her, but with Derek. It seemed he couldn't keep his eyes off her, either.

"Want to watch a movie?" Derek asked.

Sandi looked at him, puzzled. "They're showing movies . . . now?"

He laughed. "No. We've got a VCR and about a dozen films. Mostly westerns, though. Those are Dad's favorites. Maybe you don't like westerns."

"Sure I do. John Wayne. James Stewart. I love those old movies."

"Good." He took out a James Stewart cassette and sat beside Sandi on the sofa while he showed it on a three-foot-square screen. Valerie sat on the other side of Sandi, her right hand resting on Sandi's lap, ninety percent of her attention on the movie, the remaining ten on Sandi.

I don't know what it is, thought Kelly as she reclined comfortably on an armchair next to the sofa, but there's something about that girl that has really attracted those two.

Kelly felt her shoulders getting cold — she was wearing a white, sleeveless blouse and blue jeans — so she got her pink sweater out of the closet and slipped it around her.

"I *love* that sweater," Sandi said.

"Thank you," said Kelly. "Mom crocheted it for me."

"No kidding?" Sandi rose and went over to get a better look at it. "It's *beautiful*."

"Here. Try it on."

"I'd *love* to."

Sandi slipped her arms through the sleeves,

stood up, and swirled around as if she were demonstrating the sweater in a fashion show.

"It fits perfectly!" she exclaimed.

"You like it, you can have it," Kelly said.

The moment the words left her lips Kelly stared at the television screen and thought, what did I say? I *love* that sweater! It's *mine!* Mom made it especially for *me!* Now to give it away to some girl who's practically a complete stranger!

"Kelly! You're so sweet! But are you sure? Do you really . . . ?" Sandi paused, put her arms around herself, and squeezed delightedly. "I'll take it!" she cried.

Kelly found herself looking across at her brother and sister. Both were smiling at Sandi's admiring the pink sweater, as if they thought it was a nice gesture on Kelly's part to give it away.

I must be out of my mind, Kelly thought. But she couldn't ask Sandi to give the sweater back to her now. She was no Indian giver.

The movie ended at ten of eleven, and Kelly

wondered if Sandi might be thinking of returning home. After all, she'd been with them almost two hours already.

Sandi didn't seem in any hurry to return home, though, so at Valerie's suggestion, they played Scrabble. At a quarter to twelve Mrs. Roberts asked Sandi if she'd like to stay for lunch.

"Are you sure it's no bother?" Sandi asked.

"Of course it's no bother," Mrs. Roberts replied, her blue eyes twinkling behind her glasses. "One more mouth to feed is nothing. And I'm sure by the looks of you," she added, smiling, "that you wouldn't be eating us out of house and home."

It was one o'clock when Sandi decided she'd better leave before her mother started worrying about where she was.

"Call her up," Valerie cried, clinging to Sandi's arm. "Tell her you're here, and that you'll be home by five."

Sandi laughed. "Sure," she said. "And she'll have a fit." She turned to Mrs. Roberts. "Thanks a million for lunch, Mrs. Roberts. And for the sweater, Kelly. And for the movie, Derek."

"My pleasure," Derek said.

"*Our* pleasure," Valerie cut in, her broad, happy smile revealing a missing tooth.

"You must come again," Mrs. Roberts said.

"Thank you. I will." Sandi smiled at Kelly. "Again, thanks for the sweater, Kelly. I'll cherish it forever."

You should, Kelly thought. "See you," she said.

Derek showed Sandi to the door. In a minute he was back. "You must really like her, too," he said to Kelly. "That sweater was one of your favorites."

Kelly shrugged. "Yeah. It was." She headed for her room, then paused and looked at Valerie. "Just what is it about Sandi that everyone likes so much?" she asked, wondering.

Valerie shrugged. "She's just nice and friendly, that's all. Isn't that why *you* like her?"

Kelly frowned. "Yeah," she said. "Yeah, I guess so. Excuse me. I'm going to read for a while."

She went to her room and stood with her back against the door for almost a full minute, her head tipped back, her eyes closed. Why had she given that sweater to Sandi? she asked herself. After that insulting remark last night she should have shoved the sweater into Sandi's mouth!

She took a book off the shelf and opened it to the page where she had last stopped, but she just couldn't concentrate.

On top of feeling angry about the sweater, Kelly kept asking herself questions about the red sneakers.

Who had put them in her locker? Why?

Did they really make her a better athlete?

Practically everyone had said so after the game, but Kelly thought she had just been trying harder. Still, she couldn't deny she had felt different somehow — more confident.

But how could sneakers change someone? They'd have to be, well . . . *magic*. Were they *hexed* somehow?

The questions rolled and tumbled over in her mind so fast that she almost screamed.

She rolled over onto her stomach and punched her pillow in frustration. Why were the high-tops put into *her* locker? Why not somebody else's? There were other girls whose feet they must fit, she thought, and I don't need this aggravation.

This is crazy, she concluded. I'm just imagining things. She got up, went into the bathroom to splash water on her face, and went downstairs. Val and Derek weren't around. They'd gone out to play with some friends, Kelly's mother told her.

"I'm going out, too, Mom," she said, deciding to see Ester and try to get her mind off things. "See you later." She headed for the door.

"Where are *you* going?" her mother asked. "You kids seem to think all you have to do is go, go, go, and never say a word to me about it."

"I'm sorry, Mom," Kelly said. "I'm just going to bike over to Ester's. I won't be long."

"I'll give you an hour," Mrs. Roberts said. "I want you to help me with supper."

"I'll be back," Kelly promised.

She took her black-and-white three-speed bike out of the garage and headed for Ester's, who lived about five blocks away. She had barely covered two blocks when a cry came from someone on the sidewalk.

"Hey, Kelly! Wait a minute!"

She braked quickly and looked around. It was — of all people — Brett Williams.

# Seven

"How about having some ice cream?" he called, as he came running toward her. He was wearing a white sweater with the letters EMS — Eastburg Middle School — on it.

She smiled. Ester can wait, she thought. "Why not?" she said.

"Head for Louie's," Brett said, grinning broadly. "I'll run alongside you."

Louie's was a mobile concession stand about two blocks away, close to a park. And Louie — a guy with a grimy chef's hat and a mustache with needle-thin ends — was the sole proprietor.

Brett bought them each a soft ice-cream cone. They sat down on a park bench, ate, and talked about last night's basketball game.

"You played a terrific game last night," Brett said. "Better than I've ever seen you play before."

"You've . . . seen me play before?"

"Uh-huh. You were always kind of, er, slow. Anyway, you always seemed to be."

"And I wasn't . . . last night?"

"Right."

Kelly laughed, but felt flattered. "You're putting me on!"

"No, I'm not! You were good. Not great . . . but good."

Footsteps sounded on the sidewalk. It was Kelly's brother Derek with Sandi Hendrix. Sandi yelled out in a loud, cheerful voice, "Well, look who's here! Hi, Kelly!"

Kelly waved. "Hi," she said, trying to hide her dismay. Good timing, Sandi, she thought.

Sandi bounded off the sidewalk and headed toward them. "I don't think I've had the pleasure," she said, smiling at Brett.

Kelly still couldn't pinpoint why she had taken an almost instant dislike to Sandi, but right now she wished she had the courage to ignore her. "Brett Williams. Sandi Hendrix," she said.

They said "Hi" to each other.

"And you know Kelly's brother, I'm sure," Sandi said. "Derek?"

" 'Course," Brett said, throwing a quick glance in Derek's direction. "Hi."

"Hi," Derek said, not bothering to come forward. He seemed to be waiting impatiently for Sandi so that they could move on.

"Can I buy you guys a soft ice cream?" Brett offered, glancing first at Sandi, then at Derek.

"Sure. Why not?" said Sandi. She quickly sat down next to Kelly and yelled, "Derek! Come on! Brett's going to buy us soft ice cream!"

Kelly suddenly felt cheated, and one look at Derek proved that she wasn't alone in that feeling.

Derek scowled and said, "You mean you're not coming? You're going to sit there and eat ice cream?"

"Yes! What's wrong with that?"

"Wrong? Nothing! Eat all you want! I'm going!"

"Derek!" Sandi cried, jumping to her feet.

"Let him go," Brett said quietly. "I guess he doesn't like me."

"I'm sure it's not that," Kelly tried to explain, giving Sandi a meaningful look. Couldn't she see that she was interfering?

Brett shrugged and got up. "Well, anyway, what kind do you want?"

Sandi chose chocolate, and Brett left to get it.

"I'm sorry," Sandi said to Kelly when Brett was out of earshot. "Maybe I should've refused the ice cream and gone with Derek. I didn't know he would act like that."

Kelly looked Sandi squarely in the eyes. "Maybe you should have," she said.

But Sandi seemed oblivious as she glanced down at the white sandals Kelly was wearing. "You know those sneakers you wore last night?"

Kelly's heart pounded. "What about them?"

"We just came from the school a little while

ago," Sandi explained, "and I saw them on the floor."

Kelly frowned. "The locker room *floor?*"

"Right." Sandi's voice turned serious. "Maybe you'd better keep closer watch of them. *Lock* them inside your locker," she added.

"I thought I did."

"Well, you didn't."

Just then Brett came back with an ice-cream cone and handed it to Sandi. Sandi's eyes sparkled as she smiled broadly and accepted it. Her attitude changed from seriousness to cheerfulness in a split second, Kelly noticed.

"Oh, thank you, Brett! You're really kind!" she gushed.

Kelly stared at her, thinking that Sandi really knew how to twist people around her finger. She wished she had the nerve then to get up, run to her bike, and sprint for home. But she just sat there and finished her ice cream while Sandi ate hers and kept up a steady chatter at the same time.

What had she been doing at school, anyway? Kelly wanted to know. And in the locker room yet. Kelly remembered the note, "Leave the sneakers." Had she been instructed to leave them behind so Sandi could work *magic* on them?

There was more to Sandi Hendrix than met the eye, that was certain, Kelly thought.

Sandi had almost reached the cone part of her ice cream when she sprang off the bench as if something had bit her. "I've changed my mind," she said. "I think I was rude to let Derek go like that. I'll see if I can catch up to him."

Without waiting for a comment from either Brett or Kelly, she took off, holding up the balance of her ice-cream cone as she headed in the direction Derek had taken.

Brett grinned as he watched her. "Some girl. Who is she, anyway?"

"Phyllis Michaels's cousin," Kelly said. "And 'some girl' is right. If you ask me, I think she's an oddball."

Brett laughed and took a bite of his cone. "Yeah? Why do you think that?"

Kelly thought a moment before she answered. "I'm sorry. I shouldn't have said that. I hardly know her."

"That's okay," Brett said. "It's not important. Anyway, I wanted to be with you, not her."

She stared at him, holding the half-finished cone of ice cream in front of her mouth. Her stomach flopped. Anthony had never said anything like *that* to her.

"You mean that? You really like me? A short, chubby —"

"Short, yes," Brett cut in. "But who said you're chubby?" He grinned, shoved the remaining piece of cone into his mouth, and glanced past her shoulder as something caught his attention. "Uh, oh. Here comes your boyfriend," he said.

She turned, saw Anthony coming up the sidewalk, and quickly looked away. She tried to avoid Brett's eyes, but he must've seen her change of expression.

"Anthony?" she said casually. "We're barely friends."

Brett smiled and stood up. "I've got to be

going, anyway. You want to come along for a way, or you want to stay?"

She shoved the last piece of cone into her mouth, licked her finger, and got off the bench, too. "No. I've got to be going, too. My mother wants me to help her with supper."

"Fine. And take care. Okay?"

"Sure," she said.

He ran off, passing Anthony on his way.

They waved to each other, and she felt a chill ripple along her spine. What was Anthony thinking now that he had seen her with Brett? Would their friendship change?

She went to her bike. By now Anthony was close enough for him to speak to her if he wanted to. He'd be terribly immature if he didn't, she thought.

"Hi," he greeted her, his pace unchanging. "Having a good time?"

She shrugged. "Yeah," she said, and started to pedal slowly toward the street.

"Guess those red hightops really had an effect on you, didn't they?" he said.

She stared at him and almost lost her balance as the front wheel of her bicycle dropped over the curb and onto the street. Two seconds later she *did* lose her balance and had to jump off the bike before she fell off.

"What do you know about those hightops?" she asked, curious.

She saw a twinkle of amusement in his eyes as he looked back over his shoulder at her and answered, "Wouldn't you like to know?"

She could have smacked him.

# Eight

Kelly couldn't wait until the next game so she could wear the red hightops again. At first she had scoffed at the idea that she had played better by wearing them, but so many people — including Marge, Janet, and Coach Kosloski — had made cracks about them that now she was beginning to believe it. Even Brett had said, "You played a good game. Better than I've ever seen you play before." His compliment was better than everybody else's put together.

The Eagles faced the Lancers on Thursday night. Kelly had some free moments in between shots to look in the stands and twice found herself peering for someone she didn't see. Is Anthony staying away because he's mad at me? she wondered. Mad and jealous because he'd seen me with Brett that afternoon? Geez, I hope not. What's wrong with having an ice-cream cone with another guy?

Her mother and father were there, sitting with Val and Derek. They had scarcely said a word to her at home about the red sneakers, and not much more than that about her playing. They had just praised her as they always did. Whether she played a good game or not didn't seem to matter.

The game started. Amy Wallace, the Lancers' tall, dark-haired center, won the tip from Janet. Karen Truesdale grabbed it and fired it upcourt close to their basket before most of the girls realized what had happened.

"Get down there, Kelly! What're you waiting for?" Coach Kosloski's loud, commanding voice boomed through the gym. Kelly felt a twinge of embarrassment as she glanced around but didn't see the girl she was supposed to be guarding anywhere near her. A moment later she did, but it was too late then. Renee Franklin, the Lancers' swift little right forward, sprinted across the floor, caught a pass from one of her teammates, and laid it up against the boards with no one within five feet of her. The ball wobbled through the net for two points.

"Kelly! Get on your toes, will you?" Janet yelled sharply.

Kelly shook her head, exhaled a lungful of air, and reached the side of the court in time to see Fran getting ready to throw the ball in from outside of the sideline. After four quick feints, she got the ball off to Marge. Marge dribbled it toward center court, then lost it to Renee. Renee sprinted down the court toward her basket, bouncing the ball as if she had a rubber band strung to it and her fingers.

"Kelly!" Coach Kosloski's shrill voice cut through the din. But Kelly was already rushing downcourt as fast as her legs would carry her. What else did Coach want?

It was Ester who managed to stop Renee. Kelly had seen her break from the player she was guarding after realizing that Renee was running freely. She blocked her forward progress, then succeeded in getting her right hand on the ball for a jump-ball call.

Ester and Renee went toward center court and stood opposite each other, sweating and breathing spently, and waited for the ref to toss up the ball.

I'm making a monkey of myself, Kelly thought. Twice that Franklin kid broke loose as if I wasn't even around. She wondered fleetingly whether the sneakers weren't working.

A horn blatted from the scorekeeper's table. Kelly glanced in that direction and saw Phyllis Michaels running in, her eyes on Kelly.

"Out, Kelly," Phyllis said.

Kelly ran off the court, heading for the wide, empty space between two of the substitutes. But Coach Kosloski, sitting near the end of the bench with plenty of empty space next to her, motioned Kelly to come over.

Kelly sat. She picked up a towel that was within arm's reach of her and wiped her forehead, face, and neck.

Coach Kosloski looked at her. "What's the matter, kiddo? Something wrong?"

"No."

"You sure? You can't seem to get your motor started."

Kelly shrugged. "I know."

"Glad you do." The coach glanced at Kelly's red sneakers. "I'm surprised," she said.

"Why?" Kelly asked.

"Those sneakers seem to have lost their magic."

Kelly's heart leaped to her throat. "What did you say?"

"Well, you wore them in the game against the Roadrunners and played great," Coach Kosloski said. "I just thought they might make a difference in this game, too." She laughed and slapped Kelly's bare knee. "Just kidding, but it really did seem that way, I thought."

"Yes, I guess it did," Kelly agreed. She didn't want to say that that was the reason she was wearing them now.

Whether the coach was kidding or not, Kelly was sure that the red hightops really *had* had something to do with her playing. She hadn't

70

really *felt* anything at the time, except that she hadn't been *afraid*.

*Something about the sneakers had made her play without being afraid or shy*, she thought. It sounded crazy, but it was true. Or at least, that's what she had thought before this game. Her slow performance so far today made her question everything all over again.

Two minutes before the first quarter was over, the coach took Phyllis out and put Kelly back in.

Almost immediately, Kelly saw a chance of intercepting a pass from Amy Wallace, the Lancers' tall center. She sprinted diagonally across the court, caught the ball, turned, and dribbled it a dozen feet, when two Lancers suddenly bolted up in front of her. Quickly she shot it to Ester, who was running toward the basket with her guard several feet behind her. Ester caught the ball on the run, bounced it once, then leaped and laid it up against the boards. A basket.

"Nice play, Kelly!" a voice shouted from the stands.

Kelly recognized Anthony's voice. So he

71

*had* come to the game. Why do I care anyway? she thought. He'd show more interest in me if he really liked me, wouldn't he? Anyway, someone else is interested in me, now. Someone who was certainly more popular than Anthony was.

But where *was* Brett? She hadn't seen him, nor heard his voice, either.

# Nine

Seconds later the horn blew, announcing the end of the first quarter. Kelly turned and headed toward the bench, the prickling sweat rolling down the sides of her face and arms. She was breathing a little harder than normally, but she had done a lot of running and passing during those last two minutes, too.

"Thanks for that pass," a voice beside her said.

She turned to Ester, who flashed a brief smile and headed toward another section of the bench. "That's okay," Kelly answered. The two girls hadn't had a chance to talk lately,

73

and Kelly looked forward to the time she could fill Ester in on the latest developments about the sneakers — and Brett.

Kelly saw Coach Kosloski smile at her, and expected her to say something about her performance on the court. But the girls — including those on the bench — were all congregating in front of the coach, waiting for the usual between-quarters, shot-in-the-arm lecture. They all knew what to expect; they had heard it before in one form or another. But they listened anyway, looking at the coach crouched there in the middle of them as if this were the first time.

When she was finished they all seemed better prepared and eager to get in the game again to prove her right. Kelly felt the same slow-growing surge of excitement, as if the feeling were a tonic that they all got from the coach at the same time.

They had a few seconds to think about the coach's words before the horn sounded again, announcing the start of the second quarter. But Kelly wasn't thinking about her words this time. She was thinking about the red hightops. They seemed to be working just fine now. But she still didn't know why they had been given to her. Or what made them work.

"Kelly! Just a minute."

She saw Coach Kosloski motion to her. "You really played well out there, you know. I can't say that those sneakers had anything to do with it, but" — she smiled and squeezed Kelly's arm — "let's pretend they did, anyway. Okay?"

Kelly smiled back. "Sure." But she knew she wouldn't be pretending.

"Fine. Okay, get out there. But . . . play fair."

Play fair. Don't I always? Kelly thought.

She glanced at the electric scoreboard as she headed for her position near the Lancers' basket. Lancers 16, Home 13. The Eagles had some scoring to do, she thought, or find themselves biting dust when the horn gave its final blast.

Ester took out the ball and passed it in to Janet. Janet dribbled it upcourt till she got past the center line, then bounce-passed a hard one to Fran Russo, who was running up in front of her. Fran caught it, feinted a shot to the basket to fool the girl guarding her, then jumped again and took a shot. The ball rainbowed gracefully through the air, struck the front side of the rim, and glanced off toward the corner. Kelly saw that with some strong effort she could intercept it, despite two girls in orange who were rushing toward the ball, too.

She bolted after it. The ball had made its final bounce before heading for out-of-bounds, and Kelly, seeing one of the girls reaching out to grab the ball, sprang in front of her and slapped the ball back. The two girls then collided and went crashing to the floor together.

Kelly, unhurt, rolled over and then up onto her feet. The Lancer was getting to her feet, too.

"I'm sorry," Kelly said, apologetic. "You okay?"

"Yeah," the girl said. She blew back some strands of hair that had fallen over her face

and scrambled down the court. Grinning, Kelly chased after her.

She saw Janet dribble the ball to the corner, then turn and take a set-shot. The ball looped up high, dropped, struck the rim, and bounced off.

The fans groaned.

A Lancer grabbed the rebound, passed it to a loner down the court, and two seconds later the girl sank a lay-up.

"Take it out, Kelly," Janet suggested.

Kelly did. She tossed an overhead pass to Fran, who quickly passed it upcourt to Marge. To Kelly's dismay, Marge flubbed the pass. A girl in orange intercepted it, headed in the opposite direction with it, and Kelly sprinted after her, determined to get the ball.

The girl passed the ball to Renee Franklin. Renee caught it, stopped dead in her tracks, got set for a shot, and Kelly rammed into her. Hard. So hard she bounced back from the impact. Her chest ached, and she bent over, a million stars flashing in front of her eyes.

From somewhere near, a whistle shrilled,

and a voice shouted, "Blocking! Two shots!"

A strong hand grabbed Kelly's arm. "Kelly, you okay?" Janet's voice came as from a distance.

Kelly nodded. "Yes. I'm okay." She straightened and met Janet's eyes. "I'm sorry. I didn't mean to . . ." But actually, Kelly realized, I *had* meant to hit her.

"Don't worry," Janet said. "You sure you're all right?"

Most of the stars were gone by now. "I'm sure," Kelly said, and headed toward the nearest line at the keyhole where Renee Franklin was getting ready to take her foul shots.

The girl sank the first one, missed the second. Marge was there to grab the rebound and bounced it to Kelly as Kelly darted in front of her. She dribbled it toward the corner, safely away from two Lancers who had taken two or three steps toward her, then changed their minds and headed upcourt.

Finding her side of the court practically empty now, Kelly dribbled the ball toward center court, trying to decide whether to make a go for the basket or to pass it. The Lancers were playing a zone defense — protecting the four corners and the front of the basket — which made going for it pretty tough, Kelly knew. Well, no sense risking another foul, she thought. She dribbled across the center line, then quickly shot a pass to Ester, who was maneuvering back and forth and around a Lancer. The girl was protecting her zone and keeping her eyes on Ester at the same time. It was tricky defensive playing, but she was good at it, Kelly saw. Too good to consider throwing to Ester.

From the corner of her eye, Kelly saw Marge dash in front of her guard, putting herself in a free position. Kelly passed the ball to her and ran toward the basket, waiting for Marge to return the pass.

Marge didn't even glance in her direction. She dribbled once, then passed to Ester, who was rushing toward the basket.

"Here!" Kelly called to her, raising a hand, wiggling her fingers to show she was free.

Ester caught her eye, feinted a pass, then

bounce-passed to Janet instead. Janet, who was cutting across the keyhole toward the basket, caught the pass, took a long step, and went up and pushed the ball gently up against the boards. The ball rippled through the net for two points.

Kelly looked at Ester. "Thanks for the pass," she said sarcastically.

Ester looked surprised, but didn't answer.

A Lancer dropped in a fifteen-footer, which seemed to spark the team into new life. They began to sink in one after another, including a two-shot foul committed by Ester, after which Coach Kosloski took her out and put in Tootie Davis. With four and a half minutes to go in the first half, the Lancers had a comfortable lead of nine points, 36 to 27. Kelly couldn't believe it.

She saw Janet pounding the palm of her right hand against the fingers of her left — the time-out sign — and trying to catch the referee's attention. In a few seconds he saw it and blew his whistle.

"Time!" he called. "Reds!"

Breathing hard, Kelly walked off the court toward the coach's bench where Coach Kosloski was already crouched, waiting for her team. "Come on! Come on!" she ordered anxiously. "Get the lead out of your feet!"

The five girls changed their walk into a sprint, gathered around the coach and looked at her, waiting, as sweat rolled off their gleaming bodies.

"You're letting them run all over you," Coach Kosloski said, her eyes darting from one girl to the next. "Fran, you're dribbling too much. *Pass* the ball. Marge, you're taking too many long shots. That's okay if you were hitting, but you're not. So, pass, too. Okay? Janet, you're the tallest. Make use of your height. Play closer to the basket. Kelly —" Her eyes met Kelly's. "Let yourself go, Kelly. You seem to be holding back, especially after the collision with one of the Lancers. Forget it and start playing yourself again. But, safely. Okay? No more collisions."

The horn blew. Time-out was over. The team headed back onto the court.

"Kelly!" a voice called from the stands.

Kelly glanced toward the direction from which it came and saw Sandi waving and smiling at her. "Good luck!"

Kelly started to ignore her, but something else about Sandi attracted her attention: the guys she was sitting between, Derek and *Anthony*. What *nerve!* Kelly fumed. Why doesn't she get Brett to sit with her, too?

What am I doing? she suddenly thought. Why should I care with whom she sits?

"Kelly!" Janet called.

Kelly looked up and saw Janet pointing toward a girl in orange — the girl Kelly was supposed to guard. Darn Sandi, Kelly thought grimly. You'd think she had yelled at me purposely to divert my attention from the game and let me know with whom she was sitting. *I could belt her!*

It was Lancers' ball, but within ten seconds Janet managed to swipe it from a forward and take it upcourt, where she passed it to Marge. Marge bounce-passed it to Fran, and Fran leaped, feinting a shot to the basket. She

83

snapped it to Kelly who was sprinting toward the basket. Kelly caught it, went up, and dropped it through the net.

"That-a-way to go, Kell'!" a fan shouted.

The Eagles sank three more baskets and the Lancers two — plus a foul shot on Janet — when Kelly saw the forward she was guarding take a pass and head downcourt with no one in front of her. The score had reached a tie: 47–47.

Oh, no! Kelly's heart raced.

Halfway downcourt she tried to steal the ball from the Lancer, failed, and tried again. This time her right foot got in front of her opponent's left foot, and the girl tripped and fell.

Kelly stared at her, shocked by what she had done. Oh, don't be hurt! she wanted to cry out. Please, don't be hurt!

But in the next second, Kelly grabbed the ball, turned, and headed back upcourt, dribbling the ball as fast as she was able to. Could she go all the way? She wasn't sure.

She was near the basket now. One more dribble and . . .

She started to jump — raising the ball up to lay it up against the boards — when she was hit from behind. She went crashing to the floor, and pain shot through her right arm as it grazed the shiny floorboards.

From near midcourt a whistle shrilled. "Orange . . . foul!" the referee yelled.

# Ten

"You okay?" Janet asked, as she came running forward, a worried expression on her face.

"I don't know," Kelly said, rolling slowly over onto her side and then up onto her feet. She looked at her hurt arm and saw a red bruise on it. But the skin wasn't broken. "I'm okay," she said. This is really turning into a rough game, she thought wryly. But she was enjoying every minute of it.

"Two shots!" the referee called. He got the ball, went and stood on the foul line, waiting for Kelly.

She made the first shot and missed the second. There was heavy traffic underneath the basket for a few seconds as Marge and Janet tried to push the ball up against the boards and into the basket, and two of the Lancers' girls tried to get control of it. Suddenly one of the girls kicked the ball accidentally toward the sideline, and Kelly sprinted after it. She knew there were only seconds left to go in the half. But if she could retrieve the ball and take a shot before the horn blew . . .

She caught the ball just before it went out-of-bounds, turned, and bolted toward the basket. Two Lancers seemed to materialize as if by magic in front of her.

Neither one of them got any closer. They just kept their arms and legs spread-eagled in a tight-walled defense. Suddenly the ball bounced against the foot of one of them, deflected to the side, and Kelly bolted after it. At the same time one of the Lancers bolted after it, too, and both she and Kelly reached the ball simultaneously.

*Shreeeek!* the referee's whistle sounded. "Jump ball!"

The referee got the ball and stood on the foul line, waiting for Kelly and the Lancer, both of whom were brushing their hair back from their shiny, sweat-beaded faces.

"Why didn't you pass it?" Ester exclaimed from behind the Lancer.

Kelly tried to control herself from exploding. "I thought I had a chance to score a couple of points myself before the horn blew," she said calmly. She hadn't scored more than six or seven points to Ester's twelve or thirteen. What more did Ester want?

The ball went up, Kelly tapped it to Janet, and Janet fired it to Ester. Ester dribbled it down to the Eagles' basket, took a shot, and missed.

Two seconds later the first half was over. Eagles 48, Lancers 47.

"I think I'll have you warm the bench for a while when the second half starts," Coach Kosloski said to Kelly, as both teams headed for their locker rooms. "You seemed to have gotten kind of over-energetic out there."

Kelly stared at her. "I did? I didn't realize it."

"Oh, you did, all right," the coach said, smiling.

Kelly met the gaze of her pale blue eyes. "Does this mean you don't want me to wear these red sneakers in the second half?"

The coach laughed. "No. I want you to continue wearing them, all right. I just want you to sit it out for a while, that's all."

"Suppose I took them off? Wore my other ones?" Kelly asked.

"Oh, Kelly." Coach Kosloski paused and drew Kelly to the side. They were out of the gym now, out of earshot of anybody else. "Kelly, those red sneakers have nothing to do —"

"Then why were they in my locker?" Kelly interrupted, staring straight into Coach Kosloski's eyes. "Why won't the person who did it show herself? What's so secret about them if they aren't special somehow?"

"I don't know," said the coach, trying to make sense of Kelly's questions.

"Well, I don't, either. But I *know* there's something different about them. I *know*."

She didn't go on. She didn't want the coach to think she was childish to believe there was really something extraordinary about the sneakers. Maybe she had said too much already.

"You have no idea who put them into your locker?" the coach asked. "No idea at all?"

Kelly thought a moment. She actually did have an idea, but she needed more proof.

"How much do you know about that new girl who's been hanging around lately?" Coach Kosloski's voice broke through her thoughts. "You know, Sandi Hendrix."

Kelly stared at her, surprised. "She's the one I'm thinking about," she said.

The coach frowned. "Why? What makes you think she's the one?"

Kelly shrugged. "The way she acts and talks sometimes," she said, finding it difficult to give a good, concrete answer. "And she has a way of getting something from you without your realizing it until it's too late."

"Oh?"

Kelly started to explain about the sweater that she had given to Sandi, then cut herself off short. The next thing she knew she'd be calling Sandi a witch if she wasn't careful!

"You're not going to finish?" the coach asked.

"I think I've said enough," Kelly said. "Maybe too much." She turned and headed for the locker room, feeling Coach Kosloski's eyes watching her.

She wondered what to expect when she entered the locker room. Some remark about her red hightops for sure.

But when she entered the room she was scarcely noticed. Ester saw her and looked away. Is she still mad? Some best friend, Kelly thought.

She sat down on the bench in front of her locker. Her feet felt hot. She took off the red hightops and almost immediately the coolness of the room made her feet feel fresh and comfortable. Oh, wouldn't it be wonderful to play without sneakers? she thought. Even without the red sneakers!

91

The second half started with Phyllis Michaels playing in Kelly's place at right guard. Phyllis was no whiz. Not even a half-whiz, Kelly thought. In fact, she took even less chances than Kelly did. She never charged an opponent, never dove into a crowd where the ball was bouncing loosely from one player to another.

Maybe *she* should wear these red hightops, Kelly thought. Maybe they'd make *her* a better player.

But, looking at Phyllis — noticing how tall she was, her long legs — made Kelly doubtful. Phyllis would never fit into those red sneakers. Never.

Coach Kosloski didn't put Kelly back into the game until the fourth quarter. The Lancers were leading by three points, 62–59. Almost at once Kelly found herself in the middle of things. A Lancer had tried to bounce-pass the ball to a teammate. It glanced off an Eagle's knee right into Kelly's hand, and Kelly pivoted and headed back upcourt, dribbling the ball across the center line, and then coming to a dead stop as two Lancers got in front of her. She saw Janet running toward the basket from the right corner and heaved the ball to her.

A Lancer jumped in front of her, deflected the ball, and both she and Kelly sprang after it. Another Lancer reached it first and started to dribble it away. Kelly sprinted to her side, stole the ball from her, and passed it to Ester, who was running up beside her. Ester took the short pass, dribbled it toward the basket, stopped, and shot. In!

"Nice shot, Es," Kelly said, running up beside her.

Ester flashed a smile. But it was too brief, Kelly thought, to be heartfelt.

Midway through the quarter, Kelly intercepted a pass from a Lancer and headed up-court, with no one in front of her except a Lancer who'd been playing back, waiting for a situation just like that to happen. The girl rushed toward the keyhole spot, where she paused — her legs spread out and arms extended — protecting her goal. Kelly paused in front of her, still dribbling the ball, feinting to the left, the right, looking for that weak spot in the Lancer's defense. But she couldn't wait too long. Already she could hear the thunder of feet behind her, both Lancers' and Eagles'.

She feinted to the left, drawing the guard to the left, then quickly sprinted to the right, pulling the ball with her left hand. She was free; no one was in front of her. She dribbled toward the basket, went up — lifting the ball as she did so — and laid it up against the boards. Basket!

Lancers 69, Eagles 68.

Two minutes to go. Kelly caught a long pass from Marge who had taken a rebound off the Lancers' boards and headed upcourt with all five Lancers chasing after her. This time the Lancer guard had forgotten to guard the Eagles' basket, and Kelly saw her chance to sink a lay-up.

But one of the Lancers — Amy Wallace — stole the ball from Kelly, pivoted, and heaved it back to one of her teammates. Two plays later Renee Franklin sank in a set-shot from fifteen feet out.

Lancers 71, Eagles 68.

"Should've passed it, Kelly," Ester said, not too pleasantly.

Kelly's face reddened. What did Ester want? More points? Glory?

Tootie came in. "Out, Kelly," she said.

Kelly ran off the court. "Nice game, Kelly!" a fan shouted.

"Keep wearing those red sneakers!" another voice cried.

She didn't look up. She didn't acknowledge the calls in any way.

She got to the bench, sat down on the empty space near the end, and watched the rest of the game from there. Janet scored another two points after being fouled while trying to sink a lay-up. Then Marge sank two more, just before the final buzzer blew, giving the Eagles their second victory, 72–71.

Kelly was the first to head for the showers, the first to finish. She wanted to be the first to head for home, too, before anyone would start asking her questions about the red sneakers. She was tired of thinking about them, and worrying about what people thought of her.

"Hey, nice game!" Sandi cried, as Kelly

95

headed out of the building, feeling fresh and clean after the cool shower. Sandi was with Derek and Valerie, chewing gum, wearing the same blue jeans, the same tear-drop earrings.

"About time," Valerie said.

"Well, I must be running along," Sandi said. "Phyllis is —"

The gym door burst open. "Kelly! Wait!"

Kelly paused and saw Phyllis Michaels, the tall, dark-haired girl, coming toward her. "What is it, Phyl?" she asked.

"Those red sneakers. Where are they?"

Kelly frowned. "In my locker. Why?"

Phyllis shook her head. "No, they're not. I looked."

"You did? Why?"

Phyllis stared at her, saying nothing, as if her tongue were tied.

# Eleven

"Phyllis, did you hear me?" Kelly asked, looking closely at the girl. "Why did you look in my locker?"

Phyllis blushed. "It . . . it was open," she stammered nervously. "And I saw you leave the locker room without them. I just figured they'd be in there."

"So you snooped," Kelly said. "What did you want to do? Try them on?"

She looked at Phyllis's shoes as she spoke, not believing that Phyllis could possibly put the red hightops on her big feet. But Phyllis's shoes were *not* big. So her feet could not be big, either.

Before Phyllis could answer, the scene in front of her locker suddenly came to Kelly clear as day, and her eyes widened to the size of doughnuts, it seemed. "Phyllis! I remember now! I *didn't* put them in my locker! I was in such a hurry to leave I forgot! Oh, wow!" She ran to the large, double door, yanked the right one open and plunged through. She bumped into several of the girls as they were coming out and excused herself as they stared after her. Finally she reached the locker room, and then her locker, which was partially ajar.

She looked under the bench, thinking that she might have pushed the hightops under it. Nothing. Then she checked her locker, just in case. She saw her basketball uniform hanging in it, and her old, dirty white sneakers. The red ones were not there!

"Somebody took them," she said softly.

"Maybe *stole* them is more like it," said Phyllis, as she and Valerie came in behind Kelly.

"Come on," said Valerie, heading out of the locker room. "Let's get out of here. Mom and Dad will begin to wonder what happened to us."

Valerie waited for Kelly to catch up to her, then took Kelly's hand and walked with her out of the door and down the hall.

Derek was holding the outside door open for them. "Dad said they'll be waiting for us at the car," he said.

Kelly and Valerie stepped outside. The night was cool, refreshing. Amber lights on tall poles lighted the wide sidewalk. Cars with beaming headlights were driving slowly out of the parking lot. But these were vague images taking place far away as far as Kelly was concerned. Her thoughts were on the red sneakers. She couldn't get them out of her mind.

She shook her hand free from Valerie's and started to walk across the parking lot in the direction Derek was headed.

"Kelly! Watch it!" Valerie screamed.

Kelly glanced up, but not in time to avoid a car backing out of a parking place to her left. She started to turn and run, but the rear left fender of the car struck her leg and knocked her down. Fear wrenched her as she closed her eyes tightly and rolled over and over, hoping to get out of the way of the vehicle before it would run over her. At the same time loud screams pierced the night air. She didn't realize until seconds later — when the car had stopped and its driver and passengers were quickly getting out of it — that the screams belonged to her and Valerie.

"Oh, no!" cried the driver, a dark-haired young man in his late teens, as he rushed to her side. Kelly was sitting up, staring at a bump on her leg that had already turned a shade of blue. Funny, she thought, but it looks worse than it feels.

The young man peered worriedly at her through thick, gold-rimmed glasses. "I'm sorry," he said, his voice thin. "I never saw you. Are you hurt?"

"My leg was hit," Kelly said, rubbing the bump gently. "But it hardly hurts."

Derek and Valerie knelt beside her, their

faces pinched with worry. Derek examined her leg. "Just a bruise," he said. "I'll get Dad and Mom." He got to his feet and rushed away.

In less than a minute, Kelly's mother and father were at her side, examining her leg, asking her if she were hurting any place else. "No," she said.

"I'm Jim Scott," the young driver said nervously. "I still think it would be a good idea if someone called the cops and the ambulance."

"I do, too," Mr. Roberts agreed. "Will you do it, please?"

"Sure."

An ambulance came, and Kelly was taken to the emergency room at Eastburg Memorial Hospital. A patch was put on the bruise, and she was released. Jim Scott telephoned his insurance company, explaining the details of the accident, and Mr. Roberts telephoned his. There was no charge pressed against the driver. Kelly figured it was her fault, anyway. She had been too preoccupied with her thoughts and was not watching where she was going.

I'm just lucky I wasn't more seriously injured, she thought gratefully.

She lay in bed that night with her eyes wide open, staring at the ceiling, thinking about the red sneakers. Who could have taken them? Sandi?

No, Kelly admitted to herself reluctantly, Sandi had been with Derek and Valerie when the sneakers were taken. It must have been someone on the team. Someone who wanted to try them, as Phyllis had. But didn't the thief realize that she'd never be able to wear them around Kelly anyway? It didn't make sense.

And Kelly still didn't know who had given them to her in the first place. Anthony seemed to know something about them. But she still suspected Sandi — even the coach had mentioned her. Did she have special powers? There was certainly some witchery about the high-tops, she thought. I always used to freeze when I played a game. Now, when I'm wearing them, I'm like a brand-new person. I'm not a bit shy.

The thought both thrilled and worried her.

Soon she found herself sweating, so that she had to push off the top blanket. She didn't know how long she had lain there before falling asleep, but sometime during the night she must have gotten cold because when she woke up the next morning, the blanket was covering her again.

Her mother had some chores for her to do that morning — vacuuming the rooms and watering the plants — which Kelly didn't mind, especially watering the plants. They were all over the place: mums, African violets, aloe, velvet-leaf philodendron, peperomia. Name it and her mother probably had it. But Kelly loved them, too.

"Just don't squeeze," she heard her mother's gentle, warning voice behind her when she ran her fingers over the tender, velvet leaf of an African violet.

"Don't worry, Mom. I won't," she promised, putting her nose down close to the plant to inhale its sweet fragrance before she went on to water the next.

Her mother was a diabetic and had to take

insulin shots daily. She got tired quickly when she worked around the house. Kelly and her siblings never minded doing tasks their mother asked them to do.

Kelly tried not to mention the red sneakers around the house, although they were foremost in her mind. It seemed that even when she tried to get them out of her thoughts she couldn't. They plagued her no matter where she went or what she did.

After lunch she asked her mother if she could go over to Ester's. Maybe Ester would help her look for the sneakers.

"Well, good," Mrs. Roberts said. "You haven't seen her in a while. Is anything going on between you two?"

Kelly remembered Ester's coldness at the game and frowned. "Just stuff on the basketball court," Kelly said. "We'll work it out."

"I hope so. You've always been the best of friends."

Mom was right, Kelly thought as she left the house. But things had changed between them lately, and Kelly didn't know exactly why. Was it because Ester was jealous of her new playing ability?

Darn! Kelly thought. None of this would've happened if it weren't for those red sneakers.

Now she felt a little nervous about going to see Ester. But that ugly wall that had come between them had to be broken down some-time. Ester had been too good a friend to let some misunderstandings on the basketball court ruin the friendship, Kelly thought. Maybe asking Ester to help me find those red hightops will patch things up between us. Right now that was the only thing she could think of to do.

She had walked almost to the end of the block when she saw a familiar figure heading toward her from the next block. Those long, sure strides and clicking metal heels told her who it was even before she saw the dark, rumpled hair and swinging arms. Suddenly her nervousness multiplied. What was Anthony doing on *this* street, anyway? He lived on Perry, two blocks over.

She crossed to the next block, almost missing the edge of the curb with her left heel. Boy, she thought. If I had missed it I would have fallen flat on my face. Would it be red *then*.

"Hi," she said as they neared each other. Was he going to stop and talk a little, or wasn't he?

"Hi," he said, meeting her eyes directly. *I don't think I've ever seen them so blue before,* she thought.

He started past her.

"Hey, aren't you going to say anything but 'hi'?" she asked.

He looked at her. "Why should I? You're the one who's been snubbing me."

"Me?" She stared at him. "I didn't think I was."

"Oh, no? Ever since you've become a hotshot on the basketball court, and met that Brett guy, you've been acting like Queen Tut. I figured if that's the way you want it, you can have it."

Kelly stood there, too stunned to move. Why

was everyone mad at her all of a sudden? Had the red sneakers changed her that much?

He started away.

"Anthony, wait!"

He turned. "I haven't got much time," he said.

"It'll just be a minute. I'm sorry, I didn't mean to ignore you. I've had a lot on my mind."

Anthony looked down, and pretended to kick something. "That's okay," he said. Then he gave her the familiar smile she liked so much.

"Anthony, I've been meaning to ask you, do you — do you really know something about those red sneakers that I don't?" Kelly said, remembering his remark the other day.

He shook his head and grinned. "No. I was only kidding to try and get your attention. I just know that when you're wearing them you play basketball like I've never seen you play before."

Her eyes brightened. "Thanks. But now

they're missing," she said. "I'm on my way to ask Ester if she'll help me look for them."

She hoped he would volunteer to help, too. She might need all the help she could get.

"I'd help you," he said, as if he were reading her mind, "but I'm on my way to the store. Mom's got to have some stuff, and you know my mother. She's one hundred percent Italian, and wants what she wants yesterday."

Kelly smiled. "My mom's Irish, and she's no different."

The words had barely left her lips when a movement beyond Anthony's shoulders captured her eye.

"Well, how do you like that?" she said. "There's Ester now."

Ester was coming down the sidewalk at a brisk pace and carrying a box. When she was within fifty to sixty feet away, Kelly could see that it was a white shoe box.

"Hi, guys," Ester greeted them, a little more enthusiastically than Kelly expected. "Just the person I wanted to see," she added, looking at Kelly and snapping her bubble gum.

Kelly stared at the tall blonde as Ester stopped in front of them and lifted the cover off the box.

Inside were the red hightops.

"Thought you might want these," Ester said matter-of-factly.

# Twelve

Kelly stared at the sneakers, dumbfounded. "Where'd you find them?" she wanted to know. "I was going over to see you — ask you if you'd help me look for them."

Ester's eyebrows arched. "Oh? Well — it was easy. They were outside of your locker."

Kelly stared at her, confused. "Why didn't you put them in there?"

Ester shrugged. "I don't know. I think I was afraid that if anyone saw me doing that they'd think I was snooping."

"So what did you do?"

"I stuck them into my duffel bag with my

stuff and brought them home with me. For Pete's sake, Kelly! You don't think I'd want to steal them, do you? What in the world would I want with a lousy pair of sneakers that don't fit?"

"Hey, look," Anthony cut in, glancing from one girl to the other, "I've got to run." He said to Kelly, "Now that you've found those sneakers, I hope everything will be fine again. I'll see you later, okay?"

"Okay," said Kelly, hoping it would be soon.

Anthony grinned and took off at a rapid pace.

Alone with Ester, Kelly felt suddenly awkward. "Thanks for bringing the hightops," she said. When Ester didn't reply, Kelly went on, "I know this sounds crazy, but I think there's something magic about them."

Ester's eyes were glued on hers. "Why?"

"Well, people keep telling me I've been playing better. . . . Do you think so?"

"In a way, yes. You don't seem to be shy or afraid." Ester paused. "But do you really think they're doing that to you?"

Kelly smiled shyly. "First, are we still friends? I'm sorry if I've made you angry. I seem to be apologizing a lot lately."

Ester's smile broadened. "Yes, we're still friends."

"Then *my* answer is yes," Kelly said, relieved. "I think the sneakers are affecting my playing, and more." She thought about how she had almost lost Ester, *and* Anthony. "Can I leave them in the box?"

"They're yours, box and all," Ester said, handing them to Kelly. Then both girls flung their arms around each other and held on tightly, neither one of them saying a word.

Kelly turned, started to head back for home, then paused and glanced back over her shoulder. "Ester," she said, "got time to come over for a while?"

"Sure," Ester said.

They walked to Kelly's house together, Kelly holding the white shoe box snugly under her left arm. Can you beat that? she thought. Was it coincidence or just plain luck that I met Ester and she had the red hightops with her?

112

Not only that, but our broken friendship was put together and healed, too. Solidly healed, she hoped.

Kelly noticed the surprised expression that came over her mother's face at the sight of Ester, then the quick smile that immediately covered up the surprise. It was an act, Kelly figured, that could qualify her mom for the local community actress's award, something her mother — a member of the Eastburg Stage Group — had never even been a candidate for.

"She brought the red sneakers," Kelly explained, heading toward her room with them.

"Hey, wait!" Valerie called, rushing in from the living room, her black hair flying. "I've been dying to try on those hightops!"

"Val!" Kelly screamed, as her sister swiped the box from her and rushed with it back into the living room. "Val! How dare you?"

"Oh, keep your shirt on," Valerie said, plopping herself onto the floor. She took off her right shoe and slipped on a red sneaker. "Shoot. It's too big."

113

"Of course it's too big, dummy," said Kelly. "Here. Let me have it."

From the corner of her eyes she saw someone else enter the room. It was Derek. He stared questioningly at the box, and she explained to him that Ester had found the sneakers in front of Kelly's locker.

"What are you going to do with them now?" Derek asked.

"Hide them," Kelly said. She took the sneaker from Val, put it in the white shoe box with its mate, and took it upstairs. She closed the door behind her, stood and looked around the room, wondering where the best place was to hide the box. She could trust Derek, but not Valerie. Valerie might get the idea to search for them in Kelly's absence and try on *both* sneakers.

Kelly finally decided that there really was no foolproof place to hide the hightops, and if Valerie got it into her head to find them, she would. I've just got to warn her to keep out of my room, Kelly thought. What else can I do? Lock my door? Mom and Dad won't allow that.

She stuck them under a stack of sweaters in the lower drawer of her bureau, wondering, as she closed the drawer, just how long she was going to be able to keep them in there. One thing was for sure, she wasn't going to tell anybody that she had gotten them back.

Ester stayed only a few minutes, then left.

That night, after retiring to her room, Kelly took out a book — the same one she had taken out before — and started to read it again. She wasn't sleepy and thought that reading might tire her eyes. It didn't. Once again she couldn't keep her mind on the story. The image of the red hightops kept interfering, as if it were right on the page in front of her.

After reaching the fourth page and not remembering a single thing she'd read, she slammed the book shut, put it back on the shelf, and just sat there, thinking. Who was behind the red sneakers, anyway? What secret magic was there about them that made them do what they did?

At least she knew now that Anthony was innocent. Who else could be a suspect? Was Phyllis lying? Was she the one who had put the hightops in Kelly's locker? But where would she have gotten them from? From Sandi, her cousin? But why would Sandi do it? And how could she have known what size sneakers Kelly wore? Had she peeked, sometime, into Kelly's old sneakers and checked the size? It was possible, Kelly thought.

Sandi was a strange one. Kelly knew that she would never forget, and always regret, that she had given her prized sweater to that girl.

What about Coach Kosloski? She seemed to care a lot about those sneakers . . .

I'm *really* going bats now, Kelly told herself, and started to slide down underneath the covers when a sound interrupted her thoughts. She lay still, listening, and heard it again. This time the sound was distinct. The creaking stairs were giving it away.

Kelly pushed the covers aside, swung her legs off the bed, and tiptoed out of the room, holding up the sides of her oversized pj's so she wouldn't trip. Someday, she hoped, her mother would buy her a pair that would fit.

A small night-light in the hall gave off just

enough illumination for Kelly to see and descend the stairs without stumbling, making sure each step was as soundless as she could make it. The person she had heard going down a few moments ago hadn't been as cautious.

The light was on in the kitchen, and a tall, slender, black-haired man wearing green-and-white polka-dot pajamas was raiding the refrigerator. It wasn't the first time she had caught him. Operating a four-pump gas station could make any man steal a snack in the middle of the night.

Her father turned as she stepped into the room, his dark-brown eyes boring into hers, his thick eyebrows squeezing together toward the center. "What in sam hill are you doing up?" he exclaimed. "You're supposed to be sleeping."

"I know, Daddy," she said. "But I can't."

"Why not?"

Kelly shrugged. "I'm going crazy thinking about those hightops."

"Those red sneakers you've been wearing?"

She nodded. "Yes. But — I suppose they

118

shouldn't be your worry, too, should they?"

He lifted out a gallon container of milk and a box of cheese, then closed the door. "Have a glass of milk," he suggested. "The amino acid in it might help you fall asleep."

Kelly looked at him. "How come you know so much about milk?"

He grinned. "What's much about that? Anyway, I took chemistry in high school. Nothing in the book says that a future gas station owner can't get a good education."

He poured the milk for her, then poured a larger glass for himself, cut two slices of cheese from the hunk he had taken out of the box, and made himself a sandwich. "No, I suppose they shouldn't be my worry," he admitted while making the sandwich, "but they shouldn't be yours, either. Somebody just wanted you to have a pair of new sneakers, that's all."

"But who'd want to give me a new pair of sneakers? Especially red ones?"

He lifted his shoulders. "I don't know. Maybe somebody likes you, and is playing a secret game with you. Don't worry about it. You'll

119

find out who it is someday. Drink up and go back to bed. Okay?"

"Okay." She smiled, kissed him, drank the milk, and went back to bed. Her father had been no help at all. But what kind of help could she expect from him? Those red hightops were hexed. They had to be.

She closed her eyes, and felt herself growing drowsy. The amino acid must be working, she thought. Chemistry has an answer for almost everything. Maybe chemistry could have something to do with the effect the sneakers have on me. . . . Before she could mull over the question any further, Kelly fell fast asleep.

The next morning, Kelly's first thoughts were on the hightops again. I've got to get rid of them, she told herself. Magical or chemical, I don't want to have anything more to do with them. They're too much trouble. I've got to get them out of our house, that's all there is to it.

After breakfast she took the box out of her bureau drawer, placed it into a brown grocery bag, and carried it outside to the garbage can.

Derek and Valerie had gone somewhere, so they wouldn't know about it. Her father had gone to work at his gas station and her mother was piling clothes into the washer, too occupied to see her daughter stealing down the stairs with a brown bag clutched under her arm.

The large, green trash can was set alongside the house, next to the brick chimney. Kelly was about to lift up its lid when a voice cut into the early morning silence. "Hey, how you doing?"

Kelly jumped. Smiling at her from the sidewalk was Anthony, his dark hair, usually rumpled, now combed down neatly. "Oh. Good morning," she said.

He frowned. "I'm sorry. I guess I startled you." He glanced at the brown bag. "That wouldn't be the red sneakers, would it?" he asked.

She stared at him, then nodded. "Yes, that would," she said.

# Thirteen

He stepped off the sidewalk and came toward her, his forehead creased into a frown. "You're not going to toss them into the garbage, are you?"

"I was," she said, releasing the garbage cover. "Why? Do you want them?"

"No. But I don't think that you should throw them away, either. They're too —" He hesitated and shrugged. "Can't you give them to somebody?"

"Maybe I can, but maybe I won't. Maybe I'll decide to keep them, after all." She searched his intense blue eyes. "They're too what?"

He waited, thinking, before he answered. "I don't know," he said finally. "But the way you play when you wear them —" He took a deep breath, sighed, and started to head back to the sidewalk. "Do what you want," he said. "I've got to go."

"Going to the game tonight?" she called.

He looked at her. "Who are you playing?"

"The Rockets. It's our last game."

He smiled. "I'll be there."

The game started at seven o'clock. The gym was jam-packed. Grandparents, parents, brothers, and sisters — even fans who weren't that crazy about basketball — filled the gym. It was Friday night, a night out for a lot of parents who would usually take their kids to a fast-food restaurant and then to a movie. Tonight a lot of them seemed to prefer to be at the basketball game. Kelly had a good suspicion why. It was because of the red high-tops. Those who had seen them in action before had come to see them again. Those who had heard about them had come to see them with their own eyes.

123

Well, Kelly thought, glancing at the large crowd, I'm sorry to disappoint you people. I left those red sneakers at home.

After talking to Anthony this morning she had definitely decided to keep them, at least until she could solve the mystery behind them. But she didn't want to wear them this time.

The girls got into their positions on the court, shook hands, and waited for the initial jump ball. Kelly was guarding Betty McCormick, brown-eyed, dark-haired, and thin as a pencil. Kelly knew her and knew she was as wiry as she looked.

"Kelly! Where are the red sneakers?" a fan yelled.

"Yeah! We want to see the red sneakers!" another cried.

Kelly tried to ignore the calls. Maybe the fans will forget about the red sneakers after the game gets going, she hoped.

It was two minutes past seven when the referee tossed the ball up between the two centers — tall, gangly Janet Koles of the Ea-

124

gles, equally tall but heavier Ann Jordan of the Rockets. Right forward Angela Kelsey grabbed Ann's tap, shot it to Betty, and Betty headed upcourt at a fast dribble. Kelly sprinted after her, hot on Betty's heels. Then Betty was across the center line, and Kelly was alongside her, reaching out to grab the ball.

Suddenly Betty stopped, raised the ball up over her head, and glanced quickly around for a teammate to pass it to. Kelly kept jumping in front of her, swinging her arms up and down in hopes of deflecting a pass.

"Steal it from her, Kelly!" a voice shouted from the stands.

Anthony's voice.

Steal it? He must be kidding! Kelly thought. She couldn't just jump in there and take the ball. It was easier said than done. And she'd be risking a foul.

As the thought passed through Kelly's mind, Betty shot a pass over her head. Kelly turned in time to see Ann Jordan catch it in the corner, feint a shot that fooled Janet, her guard, then rush in, leap, and sink a lay-up. The Rockets' fans roared as two points flashed on the electric scoreboard opposite *Visitors*.

Kelly caught Ester's smile. "Don't worry about it," Ester said. "Just hang in there."

Within thirty seconds the Rockets scored again, with a corner shot by Betty McCormick, herself.

"Kelly! Get in there!" Coach Kosloski's voice boomed from the bench.

Kelly stared across the court, and met the coach's intense, blue eyes peering from within that framework of short, blonde hair. Maybe you think I should get those red hightops, Coach? she thought. Maybe you think I should wear them again?

Even as the thought ran through her mind a fan yelled, "Get the red sneakers, Kelly! Seems like you need them!"

"Yeah! Right!" another fan added. "Better get those red sneakers, Kelly!"

Someone else laughed, and Kelly ran down-court, following the track of the ball, but mainly trying to blot out those sarcastic remarks from the fans. The strange part of it, she thought, is that I *feel* like I want to wear the sneakers, too. It was a temptation — a *growing* temptation — that she couldn't explain. With each passing minute the urge to wear the hightops mounted.

"Kelly!" a voice shouted, catching her unaware.

She turned in time to catch a pass from Janet. Without thinking clearly, she dribbled upcourt, found her path suddenly blocked by Betty McCormick, and tried to pass to someone. Anyone. Before she knew it, Betty's hands were on the ball, yanking it away from her. In just two seconds Betty had the ball and was dribbling back downcourt. Kelly found herself staring after her, incredulous. And angry at herself.

She sprinted downcourt, too, although she knew she would never get to Betty in time; would never be able to stop the pass Betty was going to throw to the girl standing alone under the Rockets' basket. Ann Jordan caught the pass that she had to jump for, then leaped and pushed the ball up against the boards.

Again the opponents' fans cheered as two more points flashed on the electric scoreboard. By the time the first quarter ended, the score was Visitors 19, Eagles 9.

Kelly saw her teammates and the Rockets scamper off to their respective benches where the coaches were crouched, waiting to give them some on-the-spot instructions. But Kelly didn't move. The urge to wear the red hightops was still there, stronger than ever now. *She had to get those sneakers. She had to wear them.*

She looked up at the stands. In just a few seconds she spotted her father. "Dad!" she called, and waved to him. She saw him stare at her, then raise his hand. "Come here!" she said, her lips forming the words enough for him to understand what she wanted. Then she headed to the corner of the court where she waited for him. In a minute he was there, looking intensely at her. "What's wrong, honey?"

"Dad, I need my red sneakers. Will you get them for me? They're in the bottom drawer of my dresser!"

He frowned. "What's wrong with the ones you're wearing?"

"I don't have time to explain, now. Please, Daddy?"

He finally agreed. "I'll be back as soon as I can," he said.

The second quarter was one-third over by the time her father returned. He was standing by the exit door leading to the locker rooms, the brown bag in his hand, when she spotted him.

Kelly looked around for Janet, and saw her guarding Ann Jordan who was dancing back and forth under the Rockets' basket, waiting for a pass. Bea Filmore, the Rockets' springy left guard, had the ball and was dribbling it back and forth out of reach of Ester's snatching, outstretched hands. Suddenly Bea flipped it to Ann, but the hands that reached and caught it were not Ann's. They were Janet's. A roar exploded from the Eagles' fans as Janet held the ball over her head, waited for the crowd to move away from her, then started to dribble slowly upcourt.

"Janet, call time! Please!" Kelly said to the Eagles' captain.

Janet looked at her. "Time? Why?"

"My dad's brought my red sneakers! I want to wear them!"

Janet stopped dribbling, held the ball in front of her, and stared at Kelly. "You must be kidding!"

"No, I'm not! Please do it! Call time — now!"

Frowning wonderingly, Janet turned to the referee, pulled the ball against her chest and tapped the fingers of her right hand against the palm of her left. "Time!" she called.

"Time!" the referee echoed. "Eagles!"

"Thanks!" Kelly whispered, and rushed across the court to where her father was waiting for her. Quickly she removed her white sneakers, took the red ones out of the bag, and put them on.

Just as she finished tying the laces of the second sneaker, she saw a pair of familiar green sneakers step up beside her. "Kelly, you don't have to wear them," Coach Kosloski said, her blue eyes piercing Kelly's intently. "You don't need them."

Kelly smiled. "But I do, Coach," she said. "I really do."

She ran back onto the court, her smile broadening as the crowd's loud shouting and cheering filled the gym. "That-a-way to go, Kelly!" a fan cried.

"Knock 'em dead, Kelly!" yelled another.

She waited for another voice — the voice of someone whose interest and care were more important to her than all the rest of the others' combined. But she didn't hear it. She glanced into the crowd where she had seen Anthony earlier, and saw him still sitting there, leaning back, his arms crossed over his chest. The expression on his face was lukewarm, nothing like that of the crowd's faces around him.

Time-in was called, and Janet, taking out the ball for the Eagles, tossed it in to Marge. Marge pivoted away from a Rocket who tried to steal the ball from her, then lost her balance *and* the ball. Quickly a Rocket dashed toward it, reached to retrieve it. Kelly, not more than a yard behind the girl, rushed forward, too.

Suddenly her right leg slid from under her and struck the foot of the Rocket player. Both girls went down.

*Phreeet!* went the whistle. "Red's ball!" the ref called.

"Oh, no!" Ester shouted, putting her hands up against her head. "Kelly! Why did you have to put on those lousy red sneakers?"

# Fourteen

Kelly was yanked and Phyllis put in her place before the next play started.

"Kelly, here," Coach Kosloski said, motioning to her.

Kelly shifted her direction from the vacant spot at the end of the bench to the middle where the coach was sitting. "I really wish you hadn't had your father get those sneakers, Kelly," the coach said, speaking into Kelly's ear. "You should've asked me first."

Kelly avoided her eyes. "I'm sorry, but I had to."

"You think they make you a better player?"

Kelly looked at her. "Don't you think so?"

The coach hesitated, then said, "I think *you* seem to think so, and that's what worries me. You shouldn't —"

Kelly interrupted, pleading, "Please don't ask me to take them off now, Coach. I'll try to watch it the next time. I promise. Please give me another chance. Okay? I'll try my best to be careful."

The coach looked at her, thought a moment, then said, "Okay. Report in. Take Phyllis's place on the next whistle."

Both teams had scored baskets while Kelly was on the bench. The score read Visitors 23, Eagles 12.

Kelly took a moment to glance at the crowd again, at the place where she had seen Anthony sitting earlier. She suddenly realized she hadn't seen Brett Williams lately. But it didn't matter anymore. It was Anthony she liked, and now she knew he liked her.

Anthony was still there. But now she also recognized the person sitting next to him, and anger flushed her cheeks. Sandi Hendrix! Why was she always interfering in her life? Kelly's mind screamed.

She reported to the scorekeeper, then stayed crouched next to the table, controlling her feelings, as she waited for the current play to end. The Rockets had the ball, were passing it upcourt toward their basket — passing, dribbling, feinting shots — and Kelly watched, itching for something to happen so she could get back into the game. Then, a few seconds later, a Rocket overthrew a pass that landed into the hands of a spectator sitting in the second row, turning possession of the ball over to the Eagles and giving Kelly her chance.

"Out, Phyllis!" Kelly said, as she ran onto the court.

Phyllis paused, stared at her, then ran off the court.

"Take it out, Kelly!" Janet commanded.

Kelly accepted the ball from the referee, stepped outside of the out-of-bounds line, and quickly found a receiver — Janet herself. Janet dribbled the ball upcourt as Kelly shot up alongside the sideline. In the corner Janet stopped, searched for a player to pass to, and saw Kelly making a fast break for the basket.

Janet's pass was perfect. Kelly caught it, leaped, and sank the two-pointer.

The crowd screamed.

She ignored the yell, charged across the center line, intercepted the Rockets' pass, then tripped over somebody's feet. Oh, no! she thought. The whistle shrilled as the ref pointed at the Rockets' forward, Betty McCormick. "Foul on eight! One shot!"

"That-a-girl, Kelly!" a fan shouted.

"Yeah. Right. That-a-girl, Kelly," a voice echoed beside her.

Kelly saw it was Ester.

Ester! It wasn't my fault! she wanted to cry.

The ref waited for the players to line up alongside the keyhole, and for Kelly to step to the free-throw line. Then he handed her the ball.

Kelly bounced it twice, paused, concentrated on the basket, and shot. The ball looped high, dropped, struck the side of the rim, and then bounced off. Kelly looked on as Janet, Fran, and the Rockets' center leaped for the rebound. Janet caught it, tried a shot, missed, and tried again. In!

"Tough luck, but two points are better than one," Ester said.

Kelly looked at her, momentarily frozen to the court. Oh, man. Was her friendship with Ester once again on the edge of breaking up?

Suddenly she made up her mind: she could not go on like this. She might lose Ester's friendship for good — maybe the other girls', too — and Anthony's. More important, she was losing her own self-respect. And all because of the red hightops. She couldn't let that go on. She'd land up in some loony house if she did.

She looked toward the exit, saw Mr. Ripley, the school custodian, standing there like a guard, and got an idea. "Coach!" she yelled across the court. "Put someone in my place!" then hurried off the court.

"Mr. Ripley!" she cried, grabbing his hands with both of hers. "Please come with me!"

His gray eyes stared at her from beneath thick, bushy eyebrows. "Why? What's going on?" he asked.

"I'll tell you later!" she said. "Please come!"

She tugged at his hands, then released them and ran through the exit door and down the hall to the locker room. She paused at the door, saw that he was still following her, then entered the room and sat on a bench. She hurriedly took off the red sneakers and put on her old white ones.

"What are you planning on doing, young lady?" Mr. Ripley asked, staring at her from the threshold of the door.

"I want you to burn these sneakers, Mr. Ripley," she said, standing up and handing them to him. "Now! Please!"

He took them, his eyes growing wider. "Do you know what you're doing?" he said, staring at her, then at the hightops. "They look new.

Brand-new. You sure you don't want to keep them?"

"I'm sure," Kelly said, wiping the sweat off her forehead, then whipping it off her hand. "Put them into an incinerator. Burn them. Now."

He shrugged. "Okay. They're your sneakers. I hope you won't be sorry."

"I'm sure I won't be," Kelly said, watching him head for the door. Then she followed him down the hall and outside where an incinerator stood in the shadows. Mr. Ripley looked at her. "You sure you don't want to change your mind?" he asked.

"Start the fire," she ordered.

He took a cigarette lighter out of his pocket, flicked it with his thumb till he achieved a steady flame, then lowered it into the incinerator. "Papers in here will get those sneakers burning in no time," he said as if talking to himself.

In a moment, Kelly saw the flames shooting up from the incinerator, could hear them chewing furiously at the paper.

140

Gently, Mr. Ripley started to lift the sneakers over the flames, then paused as he glanced past Kelly's right shoulder. A moment later someone came up and stood beside Kelly.

"Drop them in, Mr. Ripley," a soft, calm voice said. "I should've done that a long time ago myself."

# Fifteen

"Ester!" Kelly cried, staring around at the girl whose friendship she'd been afraid of losing. "I can't believe it! It was *you* who put those hightops in my locker?"

"Yes. I'm so sorry, Kelly," Ester said, her voice on the edge of breaking. "I — I really thought I was doing you a favor. I wasn't even sure they would affect you at all, as a matter of fact. As it turned out —" She looked into Kelly's eyes, clutching her hands. "Oh, Kelly. What a stupid nut I was!" She shot a brief glance at the custodian. "Come on. I'll tell you all about it on the way back to the gym. It's halftime, anyway. We've got a few minutes."

They headed back toward the entrance of the school, walking slowly, the sound of the fire crackling behind them.

"I still can't get over this. You wouldn't believe what I have been thinking . . . Maybe this question is stupid," Kelly said, "but I've got to ask it. Was there really something *different* about the sneakers? Something that . . . well, made me play like I did?"

"Yes, there was."

Kelly stared at her, her heart suddenly beating faster. She had suspected it all the time. But, now, hearing it straight from Ester was truly a shock.

"I've known Professor McNaughton ever since Dad had introduced him to me when we first came to Eastburg," Ester said. "He's a chemistry professor at the college, but spends most of his time with wacky experiments. He fits the part to a tee. He even *looks* wacky. Anyway, I called him up one day and asked him if he would do a special favor for me." She paused.

"I think I'm getting the picture," Kelly said.

Ester nodded. "I said that my idea was crazy, and if he didn't want to try it, it was all right with me. But he laughed and said crazy ideas were his specialty. I knew they were, otherwise I wouldn't have asked him." She smiled. "So I asked him if he could invent a pair of sneakers — a really *special* pair — that might change the attitude of a friend of mine from a shy girl to a girl with some spunk on the basketball court. After that first game we played against the Bluejays, I saw how shy you were. Both on and *off* the court. So I thought —" She broke off, shrugged.

"So he invented the red sneakers just for me," Kelly said. "What did he do?" she asked, curious. "How could he invent a pair of sneakers that did what those sneakers did?"

Ester laughed. "I asked him. Do you think he'd tell me? When he dies he'll take that secret, and a lot of his other invention secrets,

144

with him. But, being a chemistry professor, I figure he must have used some chemicals. Sprayed the sneakers with them, I suppose."

"I sort of guessed as much," said Kelly.

"To tell the truth," Ester continued, "I never really believed he could do it. But when I saw you wearing them and playing like you did . . ." She shook her head. "I couldn't believe it. But, then, you started to go overboard. Almost immediately after you started wearing them. You almost had *too* much spunk," she added, grinning.

Kelly laughed. "Don't I know it! I even started *thinking* differently. And I almost lost my best friend — you!" Anthony, too, she wanted to add. "But why didn't you want me to know it was you who'd put the sneakers into my locker?"

Ester shrugged. "I don't know. I think I was afraid I might get into trouble. And maybe get Professor McNaughton into trouble, too. I thought it was best to keep it a secret. But I'm glad you decided to do what you did."

Kelly smiled. "Me, too."

Relieved now that the mystery of the red hightops was solved at last, she glanced back over her shoulder and saw that the flames were no longer leaping up as high as they were moments ago. Mr. Ripley, a lighted pipe in his mouth now, was still standing watch.

Suddenly Kelly heard the horn blowing for the start of the second half. "Come on!" she cried, grabbing Ester's hand. "The coach will wonder what happened to us!"

"What are you going to tell her when she asks about the red sneakers?" Ester said, looking worried.

"That I got rid of them," Kelly replied, easing her friend's fears.

Coach Kosloski noticed that she was wearing her old white sneakers now, instead of the red ones. "Where're the red sneakers?" she asked.

Kelly smiled. "Gone. For good," she said. She turned and sat down on the bench, ignoring the curious look the coach was giving her. Maybe, someday, she might tell the coach the whole truth about the red hightops, she thought. But not now. She didn't have the time.

Coach Kosloski let Kelly start the second half, but after Kelly missed twice in making foul shots, and fumbled a pass, she took Kelly out and put in Phyllis.

"Where are the red sneakers?" a fan shouted.

"Yeah! Put on the red sneakers, Kelly!" another fan added.

Kelly ignored the cries. It will be quite some time before the fans forget about those sneakers, she thought.

"You're a little nervous," the coach said. "You haven't settled down yet. Try to relax."

Kelly went back in in the fourth quarter and did better. She sank a twenty-footer, a couple of lay-ups, and then two foul shots after being pushed from behind by her own guard. The game ended with the Eagles winning, 64–61.

Kelly found herself swamped and praised by her parents and friends as she headed off the court, but she was interested in seeing only one person right now. The question was: was he still interested in seeing her?

Suddenly Anthony was there beside her, beaming proudly. "Hi," he said, taking her hands. "You were terrific."

She smiled. "Thanks," she said, and glanced past his shoulder. "Where's what's-her-name?" she asked.

"Who? Me?"

Kelly whirled. Before she could say another word Sandi Hendrix swung her arms around her. "You were great, Kelly!" she cried. "And you did it without those red sneakers, too!" She looked at Anthony and smiled. "See you guys!" she said, then pushed Kelly into Anthony's arms, turned, and vanished into the crowd.

Anthony laughed. "Know what?" he said. "I think she's bats."

Kelly smiled, thinking of her foolish suspicions about Sandi. "She's different all right," she said. "But one thing's for sure."

"What's that?"

"She's got good taste."

# How many of these Matt Christopher sports classics have you read?

- ❏ Baseball Pals
- ❏ The Basket Counts
- ❏ Catch That Pass!
- ❏ Catcher with a Glass Arm
- ❏ Challenge at Second Base
- ❏ The Counterfeit Tackle
- ❏ The Diamond Champs
- ❏ Dirt Bike Racer
- ❏ Dirt Bike Runaway
- ❏ Face-Off
- ❏ Football Fugitive
- ❏ The Fox Steals Home
- ❏ The Great Quarterback Switch
- ❏ Hard Drive to Short
- ❏ The Hockey Machine
- ❏ Ice Magic
- ❏ Johnny Long Legs
- ❏ The Kid Who Only Hit Homers
- ❏ Little Lefty
- ❏ Long Shot for Paul
- ❏ Long Stretch at First Base
- ❏ Look Who's Playing First Base
- ❏ Miracle at the Plate
- ❏ No Arm in Left Field
- ❏ Red-Hot Hightops
- ❏ Return of the Home Run Kid
- ❏ Run, Billy, Run
- ❏ Shortstop from Tokyo
- ❏ Skateboard Tough
- ❏ Soccer Halfback
- ❏ The Submarine Pitch
- ❏ Supercharged Infield
- ❏ Tackle Without a Team
- ❏ Tight End
- ❏ Too Hot to Handle
- ❏ Touchdown for Tommy
- ❏ Tough to Tackle
- ❏ Undercover Tailback
- ❏ Wingman on Ice
- ❏ The Year Mom Won the Pennant

All available in paperback from Little, Brown and Company